Lock Down Publications and Ca$h
Presents

GETTIN' MONEY BY THE TRUCKLOAD 2

WILDN'

Written By
CHRISTOPHER "DIESEL" HORNEZES

First Edition 2025

Printed in the United States of America

Lock Down Publications
P.O. Box 944
Stockbridge, GA 30281
www.lockdownpublications.com

Like our page on Facebook: Lock Down Publications
www.facebook.com/lockdownpublications.ldp

Stay Connected with Us!

Text **LOCKDOWN** to 22828 to stay up-to-date with new releases, sneak peaks, contests and more…

Like our page on Facebook:
Lock Down Publications

Join Lock Down Publications/The New Era Reading Group

Visit our website:
www.lockdownpublications.com

Follow us on Instagram:
Lock Down Publications

Email Us: We want to hear from you!

Chapter 1

YESSINIA

"Antonio!" she screamed, running as fast as she could towards the sound of where the gunshots had come from. "Baby! Please! Say something!"

Right behind her was G-Baby, Romeo, Tool, and ChaCha. They were all terrified out of their mind after hearing the unmistakable sound of a shotgun blasts, then gunshots from a pistol. They knew Macho was in trouble. When he had not responded on the Bluetooth earpieces that they all wore and were linked, they all feared the worst.

Macho's older brother— head honcho of the Steel City Mafia and small circle of seven they had formed with their five best friends from childhood back in their hometown of Pittsburgh, PA— couldn't fathom losing his brother. They had already lost their father, their mother, and one of their grandmothers.

Yessy had grown up with nothing but hard knocks in her life, coming up in the Southside of the Bronx. She and her brother Romeo had been through hell and back all their lives. Neither of them wanted to know what life was like without El Tiguere around.

G-Baby, a ride or die chick from Chicago, was the only one in the group that wasn't from The East Coast, but she couldn't have been more close to them if she was from Pittsburgh, like Macho and Tool, or from New York, like Yessy, Romeo, and ChaCha. They were her family. Family that she loved more than her own life. Macho was her best friend, they were as close as she and Yessy were, maybe closer. Only one person knew what G-Baby's true feelings was for Macho. Those feelings made her legs move twice as fast as Yessy's to get to him, while she prayed to the man above to not take Macho from them.

ChaCha, the matriarch of the multimillion-dollar Valdez operation, was scared shitless. She was more than just in charge of the family's massive empire, more than a gangstress from the streets of Jackson Heights, Queens—raised by a Colombian hitman and a Puerto Rican dope girl—and more than the boss of thousands of people. She was family and cared deeply for Macho, Tool, their cousins Javi, Xavier, Evelyn, and all the others in the immediate family circle. There had been too much death in the family. A day without Antonio "Macho" Tomas Valdez was like living in a world where the sun never came out.

G-Baby passed her, but she didn't care. She kept running. They all made it back to the area with tables piled high with cocaine and fentanyl. A catwalk hung high above the space. Before receiving word from the drug lab's top dog, they had snuck up on the chemists mixing deadly amounts of fentanyl with cocaine that had come from the Valdez family's distributors around Illinois—stockpiled, cut up, and set back out—to make enough people drop dead for nobody to buy Valdez coke, or for the DEA to swoop in and take the big Dominican family down.

BOOM! CLICK-CLACK-BOOM!

Yessy quickly turned her head toward the office. She and the others saw a small woman fall backward out of the doorway.

She and G-Baby took off, with the others right behind them.

As they got closer, they instantly recognized the woman and gasped in shock.

"I'm f-fine! Just g-get him outta here!" Agent Roxanne Bermudez stammered, breathing heavily from the pain of the close-range shotgun blasts that would've blown her in half if she hadn't been wearing Teflon.

Yessy screamed when she saw her man on the floor, on his back, not moving.

"Antonio!" she cried, running to him.

G-Baby and the others all gasped, but when they saw him move as Yessy crouched beside him, they were filled with relief.

G-BABY

Thank you, God. Thank you, she thought, so close to breaking down into tears.

"I'm here, baby! I'm here! Can you move?" she heard Yessy cry.

A noise caught G-Baby's attention. She looked to the rear of the office and noticed a door was slightly ajar.

Without a word, she took off for it, yanking it open. She saw a long corridor with an open doorway at the other end.

"Gabi, wait, ma!" she heard ChaCha holler.

She ignored the queen of the family and, with her Sig Sauer MPX—with a custom-made 50-round clip and sound suppressor screwed into the barrel—ran toward the other end, hoping to catch whoever she was sure had tried to take Macho's life.

She reached the other doorway and saw it led to an outer area with an alley. She heard an engine start up as she stepped out.

Running toward the sound, G-Baby saw a Cadillac Escalade peeling off down the narrow alley toward a street.

She took aim at it and fired at the rear window. It exploded, but despite continuous shots into the SUV, the driver reached the end and hit a hard left, disappearing from her line of sight.

"Fuck!" G-Baby shouted.

Tool and Romeo ran out just then, assault rifles in hand.

"Whoever it was got away," she told them, beyond pissed at herself for missing—with years of military training deeply instilled in her that made her both a fearless goon and a soldier.

Tool grumbled to himself. "It's not over. They know my brother ain't dead, so we'll be seein' the pussy muhfucka again," the massively tall dreadhead said. "Come on. If that bitch is here, she came to work—and I bet her punk-ass buddies are close by."

Tool led them back inside. G-Baby was relieved to see Macho was up. His woman and ChaCha had him by his arms, helping him walk. The DEA agent had managed to pull herself up from the floor and peel off her DEA polo shirt. Her buckshot-riddled bulletproof vest was exposed. She looked hurt.

Ignoring her, G-Baby, Tool, and Romeo left the office, hurrying to get out of the building before it was crawling with more DEA agents.

AGENT BERMUDEZ

The Cuban woman watched her target being helped out of the office. She had half a mind to grab her gun and do what she had followed Macho Valdez to do, but when she heard a groan, her focus left the Valdez posse and shifted to the man who had been on the floor when Macho was shot by the masked gunman—whom she had popped so many times with her Glock 9—only to discover that, like her and Macho, he was wearing body armor under his baggy hoodie.

The discovery that her bullets hadn't had any effect on him had rattled her—enough that the guy had been able to spin on her and shoot her twice, pushing her backward out of the office.

The man in the suit looked up at her, then around the office.

"Wh-what… happened?" he asked.

She limped over to him, holding her bruised chest with her left arm and her service pistol with her right.

"Your friend shot me after I popped his ass. You're running an illegal drug mixing operation that's responsible for hundreds of overdoses around Illinois. And for that, you pulled a gun on me and tried to kill me—when I came in to bust you," she said. "Then you died."

"Wh-what the hell are you—"

BOCKA!

Roxanne silenced Corona Acevedo with a bullet to the temple, splattering his brains all over the carpeted floor.

She pulled her phone out of her pocket and made a call.

"I'm shot. I need assistance. Offender down, one in the wind," she said, adding her location before ending the call.

Roxanne sighed to herself. She sank down to the floor and lay on her back, waiting for her team to arrive. As she looked up, she saw his face—the face of the drug-trafficking kingpin she wanted both to arrest and charge with everything she could, while also finding Macho Valdez, taking him somewhere secluded, and enjoying another hot and steamy night with him like they had back when she thought he cared.

At the time, she'd been trying to infiltrate his world—not realizing the wild sex tape he had made of them, unbeknownst to her, would end up on her boss's desk. But the blessing she'd gotten out of that failed undercover mission…

She only wished she could somehow get the chance to tell Macho—but she was terrified of how sure she was about how he'd react.

And if it ever got back to her boss, she wouldn't just be put on desk duty again—she'd be unemployed.

Chapter 2

MACHO

Hours later...

"Antonio! Stoooop!" Yessy urged as he again went to get up from the couch in their big living room.

"Macho, come on, bro, just chill," Romeo added.

ChaCha, Tool, and Romeo all stood to assist the Nuyorican in keeping the Steel City Mafia good down.

Off to the side, whimpering as they felt Macho's pain, Yessy's big German Rottweiler, Maliante, and Macho's bulky chocolate red tiger-striped Red Nose Pit Bull, Dreams, stood side by side, saddened by their human's pain. With them, ChaCha's huge brindle-turned Presa Canario, Pable, sat as tall as a mini horse, and close to her sire was Tool's puppy Rottweiler, Angel.

"I'm cool, yo. For real," Macho swore. "If I lay down, the shit's gon' tighten up on me. I gotta move around."

Yessy relented and let her big six-foot-three-inch Dominican–Puerto Rican beast up. He looked down at his five-foot-nine-inch-tall caramel-brown Boricua goddess and smiled at her.

"See? I'm good. The body armor did the trick."

They all saw the big blush across his toned six-pack abs. Yessy shook her head. It horrified her to think about just how close he had come to death. Even though he was up and smiling, her eyes welled with tears.

"Hey, hey, hey, amor, no llores." Macho pulled his woman to him, wrapping his massive arms around her.

"Can't nobody get me out the way, bae. They call me El Tiguere for a reason. Best believe, though, on my mama, I'ma get that nigga, yo. Homiez."

Tears. Macho held her close to him. He saw the others were all looking relieved but upset as well. Then he realized he didn't see G-Baby.

"It's okay, amor. We're good," he assured his woman.

For the next thirty minutes, they all sat together in the living room. Yessy stayed at her man's side, feeling safe and happy that he was still here.

Tool and Tamalita said goodnight, then made their way upstairs to one of Macho and Yessy's guest rooms. ChaCha hugged Macho, kissed his forehead, then did the same with Romeo and Yessy before taking her dog and hopping into her custom Fendi-monogram painted Lamborghini Centenario Roadster to head home.

Romeo headed up to one of the other bedrooms to get some sleep. Macho carried his woman to their bedroom, with their dogs and Angel following.

Yessy yawned, exhausted, as he laid her down on their bed.

"Baby," she called to him softly as he undressed her.

"Dímelo," Macho said.

"I finished. I'm discharged," Yessy informed him.

"Word? My baby's a civilian again?" he asked with surprise.

She nodded. "Time to put those..." she paused and yawned again, "plans into action."

Macho watched her close her eyes, and in an instant, she was knocked out.

He smiled at the sleeping beauty. Leaning down, he kissed her lips, then pulled the covers up over her.

For a minute, he gazed at her. He was proud of her. Yessy had been through so much—the type of shit that plenty others had committed suicide from. The woman she fought to become was so honorable and admirable to him. He only knew one other woman who had been through hell and came out of it like a straight soldier.

"Watch over ma, okay?" Macho said to the dogs.

Maliante jumped up on the bed, followed by Dreams and Angel. They plopped down on the bed close to Yessy, surrounding her.

Macho headed out of the bedroom and made his way to G-Baby's room.

The lights were off when he entered. He heard soft R&B music playing. On her bed, G-Baby was curled up, facing the window. Macho walked over to her and saw that her eyes were closed.

He leaned down and kissed her forehead, silently thanking her for being such a rider.

He left the room, pausing in an upper lounge area. A thought came to his mind.

He had to know why. He had to.

Macho got his phone out and called his cousin.

"Yo! Cuz, you cool?" Javi answered right away.

"Yep, I'm Gucci. I need a ride, though. Come scoop me."

"Where you at?" Javi asked.

"Crib."

"I'm on the way. Be outside, cuz."

The call ended. Macho went and found he still had some Vicodin from the last time he had been seriously injured. He popped a 750 and washed it down with a shot of Patrón. Putting on another tank top, he grabbed his phone and snuck out of the house just as Javi's purple McLaren P1 turned down his street and came to a stop next to him.

G-BABY

She watched him get into Javi's car from her window, then watched as the exotic hypercar rolled off. She sighed to herself, wishing he would just stay in for the night. She was so filled with dread over almost losing him that she had cried herself to sleep. The touch of his soft lips on her forehead had woken her up, but she had played sleep, still hearing him make a call to someone to pick him up.

"Please come back, Antonio," G-Baby said as the McLaren disappeared from her line of sight.

AGENT BERMUDEZ

"Fuck!" she cursed as she entered her modest single-level home in Zion just before one in the morning.

Roxanne was beyond pissed that she had failed once again to get Macho Valdez off the street—whether straight to a jail cell or into her bed.

She kicked off her black pumps and walked on stocking feet through her living room, heading for the kitchen. She needed a strong drink, then another, and another, then one more before downing a beer.

After the big scene at the drug lab, Roxanne's boss had gone apeshit on her. He received a call from crime scene techs saying her story wasn't matching up. She had told other field agents what happened... her version, but the techies were disputing it. Her boss told her if it was proven that she had again violated protocol, she was done.

In the kitchen, Roxanne grabbed the bottle of Havana Club out of a cabinet and a shot glass. She poured a shot and downed the liquid fire. She poured another, tossed it back, then another, and another, and another.

The strong liquor had her burning so good. She felt sooo much better. Pausing, holding the bottle and shot glass, Roxanne's mind trailed off as his face infiltrated her thoughts.

His eyes, his smile, his thuggish demeanor had her nibble on her bottom lip. Thoughts of that blazing hot night she had given it up to him came back to her. She wanted to do whatever it took to get him to trust her, but when he slipped up inside of her, Roxanne had quickly gotten addicted and hadn't stopped craving more of him since then.

Moisture started building between her legs, soaking her panties and pantyhose. Her temperature rose—he made her hot, and he wasn't even there.

"Goddammit! Get out!" she yelled. "Get the fuck outta my head!"

She slammed the bottle down on the floor. The bottle bounced—the thick glass too tough to shatter on linoleum tile.

Cursing, Bermudez grabbed an MGD out of her fridge, popped the top, and took a huge gulp. She walked past the rum bottle, reentering her living room.

En route to the hallway to get to her bedroom, Bermudez paused when she looked at her steel-framed, glass-shaped coffee table.

Photos in stainless steel frames stood on it. She sighed, picking one up in particular and looking at it. She couldn't help but smile at her little man. His brown skin was gold, his hair was four shades of brown and curly. His smile was infectious. He looked so happy, sitting on the swing at the park she'd taken him to that summer.

"Hey, papacito," Bermudez cooed to the photo, touching his face with her finger. "Mommy misses you so much."

Tears filled her eyes as she remembered how her mother and father demanded she give Manuel to them, or they'd take her to court for custody—and win—since Bermudez was at work more than at home to raise her child.

But it was hard for her. Hard for her to look at her son. He looked just like his father. Manuel even had those jaw-droppingly beautiful blue-gray eyes.

She set the picture back down, then made her way to her bedroom, tired, fatigued, exhausted beyond belief. She needed to rest her mind and her body.

Entering her cozy bedroom, Bermudez swallowed the last of her beer, setting the empty bottle on the tall dresser next to a bunch of other empty bottles and cans.

Turning the light on, she sighed—then suddenly heard a noise come from behind her.

She shrieked when she felt a hand touch her shoulder. Grabbing her holstered gun, Bermudez ran forward, then spun, cocking and pointing her cannon at the intruder. When she saw who had broken into her home, her jaw dropped.

She wanted to squeeze the trigger and put all thirteen rounds in him, but more than that, she wanted to toss the gun and jump his bones.

"Wh-what the fuck are you doing in my house, Valdez?" she demanded.

He smirked at her, then took a step toward her.

"No! Stop!" Bermudez yelled, both jittery hands gripping her gun. "Don't come any closer or I'll fucking shoot you!"

He kept coming, kept smirking. Bermudez kept backing up, shocked that he didn't seem hurt at all from getting shot.

"Valdez! Stop! Freeze!"

He kept stepping toward her, his hypnotizing eyes locked onto hers.

In a flash, Roxanne found herself against the wall. Though she still had her gun trained on him, he stepped so close that the barrel touched his chest. His massive frame dwarfed her petite five-foot-seven-inch-tall one.

"Valdez," she cried, closing her eyes, tears squeezing through her eyelids.

"Abre los ojos, Roxi," she heard him say.

In a million seconds, his deep voice had her aroused, wanting to hear it again. She opened her eyes, looked up into his, and nearly melted.

He slowly reached up and took her gun. He set it on the table next to where they stood, then looked down into her eyes again.

"Escúchame bien, little mama," he said. "I appreciate you stepping in and helping a nigga out, but you could've gotten killed."

"You got shot too, Valdez!"

"Soy un gangsta. It's part of the game, unfortunately. Leave your overzealousness to get me here at home next time you go to work. Next time, you might not be so lucky."

"Neither will you, goddammit! What the fuck makes you think you're untouchable, huh? You and your fucking lady? He got away, Valdez! He will try to finish you!"

She saw his eye twitch when she spoke of his woman. It spooked Roxanne. She knew what he had done to people for his woman.

"Déjame a mí y mi mujer tranquilos, o vas a ver cómo este tiguere y la boricua mala meten manos," he told her. "And as far as dude goes, he's on borrowed time, shortie."

The threat flowed so swiftly out of his mouth that all hope of him ever being hers again—even for a night—vanished.

She tried to speak, but the dread he filled her with had stolen her words.

"I'm goin' back to my family. Big day tomorrow. If I even think you're watching me, I will be back."

He turned to walk off. Roxanne stayed silent until he got to the doorway.

"A-Antonio."

He stopped, hearing her call him. He turned his head a little, avoiding eye contact, but he was listening.

"I... he's..."

She couldn't find a way to say it, out of fear of him flying off the deep end.

He waited five more seconds for her to say something. When she didn't, he stepped out of her bedroom.

Roxanne listened to his footsteps. She heard them fading away, then a door opening and closing. After she heard the sound of what seemed like a race car speed off, Roxanne broke down and cried her eyes out.

Chapter 3

G-BABY

A Week Later...

"What?" she answered when her on-again, off-again lover called for the fourth time.

"Bitch, don't be answering my call like you crazy!" snapped Nya, a Moroccan belle that G-Baby and Yessy had in their unit when they were both lieutenants in the Army—and that G-Baby had gotten in bed with a few times.

Click—

"Mámate un bicho, pendeja," G-Baby grumbled as she grabbed her stuff to go get showered.

YESSINIA

"Sssss... oooooo, Antonio... yeeesssss! Lono, papi!" Yessy moaned, rubbing her own succulent 36DD breasts while she enjoyed the blissful oral her man gave her in their big glass and marble shower.

Her back was against the marble-tiled wall, her right leg up, foot resting on his shoulder. Hot, steamy water poured down on them from the "Rainbow" shower ceiling.

From the MBL:101 Xtreme home audio system, Ciara's *Body Party* crooned, serenading them.

Macho sucked on her clit, swirling his tongue around it at the same time. Yessy trembled like a volcano, ready to erupt at any moment. He pleased his woman so good, slurping and sucking on her like she was a juicy mango.

"Ay, Dios mío, Antonio! Fuuuck!" Yessy cried out loudly, feeling it coming on strong, as Cardi B's *I Like It* featuring Bad Bunny came on.

Macho took her all the way up and made her explode less than a minute later. He drank her juices as she flowed into his mouth.

He stood then, his thick 10-inch cock throbbing, ready to dive into her wetness. Yessy had her own plans before she let him enter her kitchen.

Pushing him against the wall, she sank to her knees before him and planted a kiss on the bulbous tip. She looked up at him, made eye contact, and began kissing and licking all up and down his shaft.

Macho groaned, toes curling as she took his balls into her mouth, sucking while jerking his cock with one hand.

He cursed repeatedly, eyes rolling to the back of his head. He felt her release his balls, then felt her engulf him, going balls-deep, taking him to the back of her throat.

"Fffuuuuuck! Carajo, mami! ¡Mamamelo bien, cabrón!"

Yessy spit his dick out, and still with a hand wrapped around it, stood wearing a smile so seductive Macho almost popped off in her hand.

"Ya tú sabes lo que quieres, papi," she purred. "Ponlo en este culo bien rico," she told him, making her juicy ass clap for him.

"Shheeeit, you ain't said shit but a word, bellaca," Macho said, so ready to slide in between those phat, juicy, wet Puerto Rican booty cheeks.

Yessy bent over in front of him, released his cock, and grabbed her cheeks. She opened up, exposing her brown eye. Macho, gripping his dick, marveled at the puckered pleasure tunnel. He leaned down and kissed her asshole, stuck out his tongue and licked around the rim. Feeling her shake, he stood back upright and slapped it with the bulbous tip.

She bit her bottom lip as she felt him ease into her ass. The song changed to Bun B's *Put It Down* featuring Drake.

Yessy moaned, cursed, called out his name as he fucked her. She loved how dirty and freaky anal sex was. For pleasing him, there wasn't anything she wouldn't do. And for her, the sky was not the limit.

Macho took his woman higher in her world of ecstasy until she exploded again. Feeling his dick pulsating inside her, hearing his guttural grunting, she knew he was about to cum.

Quickly, she reached back, pulled him out, and spun to face him, dropping back down on her knees. She inhaled his hardness and sucked him until he exploded in her mouth, roaring like a wild animal as she milked him for every last drop.

"Woooooooo! Shit!" Macho shouted over Lil' Ru's *Nasty Song*. "Yo ass be tryna cripple me, Yessy! Damn!"

She swallowed his cum, then burst out laughing at him. He took her hand and helped her up from the marble-tiled floor.

"So you can't handle how I do anymore?" she asked.

"Naw, I ain't say all that," he replied. "I'm just saying—fucking around with you, I'ma be the only man in human history to bust a nut so big that my spine breaks."

Yessy laughed her ass off and grabbed his dick again.

"No!" He jumped away from her. "¡No me toques, huele bicha! I'm sensitive right now!"

"Aww! Haaaa! Yeah! Got 'cha ass runnin', muhfucka!" she teased.

"Sure ya' do, punk," he replied, letting her have the win... for the moment.

"I need to take those wet-ass braids out of your head and get you looking like the man I'm proud to call mine," Yessy told him, then took his hand and led him to a bench against the main wall of the shower to take his long cornrows out.

G-BABY

"Oooooooweeeee! Lil' mama bad as hell, joe! Chsching, budda-muthafuckin' bing, biatch!" G-Baby said as she checked herself out in the tall mirror again.

Trai'D's *Gutta Bitch* blared from the speakers in her big California walk-in closet. The ensemble she had chosen for the gathering at ChaCha's—G-Baby couldn't wait to show off. It clung to her like a second skin, accentuating her curves and letting all that ass show. It was a custom design by FeFe Couture, a budding fashion line created by the girlfriend of Macho's Steel City Mafia brother—who was also like a sister to her and Yessy.

Her hair was done up, a light layer of makeup and icy jewelry shined in her ears, around her neck, wrists, and ankles. She smelled like jasmine, one of her favorite scents.

She turned sideways and looked at how phat her badonkadonk looked. Leaning over, G-Baby started making it clap.

"Click!" she shouted, making the mirror capture her image perfectly.

Taking a few more flicks—enticing enough to give the Pope a boner—G-Baby viewed them on her iPhone.

"Now that is a baaad, baaad bitch!" she said just as her phone started ringing.

A picture of Macho, with his arm over her shoulder, and Yessy's—the three of them standing in front of the Shamu exhibit at SeaWorld—popped up. Smiling, she answered his call.

"Bring ya butt on, Gangsta Boo," he said. "We outside."

"Here I come," she replied and ended the call.

Grabbing her sharkskin Birkin bag, G-Baby hurried on her sexy 6-inch pumps to get outside, where her homies awaited her.

MACHO

"Antonio, noooo, come on, bae, stooop!" whined Yessy as he held her up against the wall, begging her to let him crack.

He was dressed in a distressed denim jean and jacket fit by Balmain. On his feet, all-white custom-designed Balmain

X Nike Air Force 1s. A long white gold Cuban link chain, embedded with flawless diamonds, and a diamond Steel City Mafia charm hung around his neck. Flawless diamond studs in his ears, a white gold Richard Mille on his right wrist, and a pinky ring completed the look. Yessy had washed his hair, blow-dried it, then greased his scalp before giving him four neat angular cornrows and a razor-sharp hairline and beard line-up. His Versace cologne smelled so good, he wanted to kiss himself.

When Yessy emerged from their huge walk-in closet, rocking a blue suede long-sleeved FeFe dress—a backless design with a low cleavage line, ankle-length hem, and slits up the front of her legs to her upper thighs—Macho's eyes bugged wide like Bugs Bunny when he first laid eyes on Lola.

Her hair was spiral curled and pulled high into a ponytail, her edges gelled down and styled to accentuate her beautiful face. Diamonds flicked in her ears, in the two white gold necklaces around her neck, the rings on her fingers, and in her custom Chanel watch. Her eyelids were dusted with eyeshadow matching her skin-tight dress, lined in black eyeliner. Her lips glossed like blue chrome, shining like the "Bad Rican" charm on one necklace, done up with blue diamonds.

She was smoking, but what had her man yearning for another round was when she stepped out of the walk-in and he could see she had slid her shapely bottom half into a pair of blue fishnet pantyhose. With the dick-teasingly sexy hose, she had slid her size 7 feet into a pair of shiny white pointed-toe Christian Louboutin pumps.

Macho was a fiend for women in pantyhose and white stilettos. Red was cool, but the way white made all skin tones pop even more, he couldn't resist his woman when she put them on.

"Come on, you horny mutt! Put me down!"

"I don't wanna!" Macho said, with a dick throbbing so hard it hurt. "Yo ass knew fishnets and white heels was gon' do that to me! Why? Whaaaaahaaa-whyyy?"

Yessy laughed so hard at his theatrical acting that tears filled her eyes.

"Yooo, on my motha', you are mad wild, Antonio! Put me down, man! We're already late, pa!"

"So? I don't give no fuck!" he said, looking up at her, praying she would give in.

"Damn, bellaco!" Yessy again told him.

"Yo ass bogus, man. Homiez."

Yessy reached up and patted his face. "Aw, don't cry. You'll be okay. Now call Gabi Poo and tell her to be outside."

With that, Yessy sauntered off to go get her new FeFe bag and iPhone. Macho's eyes followed her juicy apple bottom, shaking his head. He pulled out his iPhone and called G-Baby. When she answered, he told her to be ready in five minutes, then ended the call.

YESSINIA

Cutting through the garage, between her brand-new black Mercedes S650 Maybach and Macho's white Bentley Mulsanne, where G-Baby's blacked-out Suzuki GSXR also was, Yessy pointed a key fob and pressed a button. Macho hopped into her matte black special-order Brabus edition G63 AMG Mercedes 4X4 Squared truck and moved it over, parking it behind his Mulsanne.

Yessy's Maybach rose up when the hydraulic pistons under the concrete pad it was parked on were activated by the remote. The secret hideaway parking space under the Mercedes concealed her very rare and very fast 2013 dark tangerine-colored Pininfarina Gran Lusso Coupe edition BMW M7. Macho had gotten the big-body Beamer for his woman a couple of years prior, dropping a couple hundred grand short of a million for it. Nobody in the entire Midwestern region had one.

Yessy hit another button. The twin-turbo V12 engine started up, sounding so powerful through the monstrous blacked-out exhaust pipes. Another button made it back out of the garage on its own.

Macho opened the driver door for his woman and held her hand as she slid into the exclusive back, tangerine, and M-series carbon fiber trimmed interior. Hopping in next to her, Yessy closed the garage, backed out of the driveway, and made their way through the big subdivision that Macho had built from bare ground up and gifted to Yessy—essentially giving her more than eighty luxury homes. She shared them with G-Baby and got certified as a residential real estate agent. That flowed into commercial real estate, then they took the money from the sales and started a big demolition company, which merged with Macho's trucking business.

She headed around a half-circle street lined with more houses, arriving at G-Baby's deluxe home minutes later.

"Well damn. She tryna catch something wearing that," Yessy said, pulling into G-Baby's driveway, where her purple and black Hennessey HP1000 edition SRT8 Jeep Cherokee sat parked.

MACHO

Good God Almighty... Gabriela is... damn, yo.

Macho's eyes went wide as he laid them on G-Baby in her super tight, yet sophisticated dress. It was pea green with sunflowers all over it. It had a low cleavage line, a slit up the middle, and an open back. The hem of her FeFe dress went down to her calves, allowing some leg to show. Down on her feet were bright yellow pointed-toe pumps. Her hair and makeup had her looking like she had gone to a salon, instead of dolling herself up on her own, and she sported yellow-gold Chanel jewelry in her ears, around her neck, wrists, and fingers.

"She's bad, right?" he heard Yessy ask, as G-Baby made her way towards the car.

Macho turned and looked at his woman. He saw her staring at him with an unreadable expression.

"Yes," he answered.

He saw her eyebrows rise, shocked by him admitting it.

"So... you're attracted to Gabi?"

"What heterosexual man wouldn't be, Yessinia?" He looked back at where G-Baby was taking baby steps in her high heels. "She's a peach, baby, and a muhfuckin' G. But so are you, and ChaCha, Michelle, Gloria, Nena, Vanessa... sheeeit, the list goes on and on, bae."

"You didn't say Eve, though," Yessy added, just as her bestie reached the car.

"You got me all the way fucked up if you really think I'ma say my baby cousin is sexy, yo."

Yessy busted out laughing as he opened the door and got out to greet G-Baby and assist her into the car.

"That's how you feel for the night, Gangsta Boo?" Macho asked, not even attempting to hide he was digging what he saw—more than watching Nicki Minaj walk up the steps on *Barbershop 3*.

"Why you say that? Too sexy for ChaCha's gathering, or not sexy enough?"

"Girl, you gon' have all eyes on you when we get there," Yessy hollered out to her.

"Agreed," Macho added. "Hop in so we can go. And you might wanna put your seatbelt on, too."

G-Baby chuckled, knowing the only person as crazy behind the wheel as Macho was Yessy.

She got inside and hugged Yessy, kissing her cheek. Macho closed the door, then looked up at the dark sky.

Please. Can you let it happen just once, my nigga? Got me in the rarest BMW on earth, with the two baddest Boricuas ever. Do me a solid, God, and let me experience how it would feel to crack my lady and G-Baby at the same time... Sorry for lusting, but you started it, creating sexy women like them.

"Antonio! Come on, man! What is you doing?" asked Yessy.

He got in the car and closed the door. "I was praying for a miracle, baby."

Yessy shook her head, then pulled off, heading to leave out of the subdivision.

Tool's Range Rover Autobiography was parked at the top of their street. After Yessy passed him, he turned behind her and followed her onto Green Bay Road.

Yessy got to I-94 and floored it. Macho and G-Baby flew back into their seats as more than seven hundred horsepower was unleashed. Macho managed to turn his head and saw his woman gripping the wheel with just her left hand, gangster leaning like the speedometer didn't say she was pushing more than one hundred and fifteen miles an hour.

Macho's eyes shot back to the right, looking in his mirror. His brother was nowhere in sight.

His phone buzzed in his pocket as he continued to hold on for dear life. Yessy let off the gas after a mile. He got his phone out and saw a text from an unknown number:

What up, my nigga? Just wanted to let you know that I know you're still alive, but I will finish the job.

Macho shook his head and started typing a reply:

Let me guess...this is the so-called Demon?

He sent it and got a reply seconds later:

You bet your ass it is. What do you want on your tombstone?

Macho chuckled.

Ya'mama, he typed, then sent it.

Yessy reached over and turned up the music when she heard Wiz Khalifa's "Smoking, Drinkin'" coming on. It started pounding from the three 12-inch P3 Punches in her trunk when the beat dropped.

Macho got a reply a minute later:

You a dead man, bitch.

Macho laughed to himself. He typed up another reply and sent it.

"What are you laughing about over there?" Yessy asked, turning down the music.

Macho gave her his phone. She slowed down significantly, enough to take a few glances at the messages to tell her man was in danger.

"Antonio! That shit ain't funny! Who is that saying those things to you?" she asked, handing him his phone back.

Macho felt G-Baby's presence after his girl seemed to be panicking.

"That bitch-ass nigga El Demonio," he said, "who somehow got my number."

"He knows you, Macho," G-Baby surmised. "Dude knows who you are, and he might know where you lay your head—which is next to Yessy's."

"Yeah, Antonio! Stop texting him!"

"Okay. Last one," Macho said, then typed one more reply:

I would love to keep playing text message wars, but that shit's for punks. Just pull up on me when you grow enough balls to face me. Until then, byebyebye.

He sent the message, and knew one would be coming.

A reply came seconds later:

Don't even trip. We definitely gonna handle it very soon, pussy. You fucked with my business, and now, you will pay.

Waving it off, Macho refused to acknowledge the clown any further. He tucked his phone away and sat back, tuning into Gucci Mane's "She Likes Me," featuring Yo Gotti.

Chapter 4

A little under an hour later, Yessy arrived in Chicago. She hopped off the E-way and headed to Wabash. Reaching it, she made another turn, and minutes later, she pulled into the big half-circle area where valet drivers busily took the wheel of multiple luxury and exotic cars.

Pulling up behind a glossy emerald-green Mercedes C63 AMG, Yessy parked and grabbed her tote bag. A valet walked up with a pleasant smile, ready to take her vehicle and park it in the underground section of the 100-story condominium building.

Yessy, her man, and G-Baby hopped out of the Beamer, and had all eyes on them. Taking Yessy's hand—and G-Baby's—Macho escorted the beautiful brown queens inside.

At the top floor, the gold-trimmed glass elevator doors opened up, revealing a penthouse suite so luxurious an A-list actor would offer over the $10.5 million dollar price tag to own it.

Men in expensive threads, dripping hard, joined by gorgeous women in sexy ensembles worthy of a Paris runway, filled the place. Crystal flutes of champagne were in most hands. Smiles and laughter mixed with music coming from a live DJ, playing the hottest hits of the year. The 1,900-square-foot space had a festive vibe. It was a celebration, and though random get-togethers were common in the Valdez family, Macho, Yessy, and G-Baby were still curious about the urgency ChaCha had when demanding they be there.

The elevator opened behind them again. Tool and Tamalita, both looking BET Awards-worthy in Louis Vuitton and diamonds, stepped off and joined Macho and the Boricuas.

Already there were drivers and mechanics from Valdez Transport, owned by Macho and Tool's younger cousin Javi. Everyone from Numero Uno was present, and a large group from the Kilbourne PJ & D Transport yard—ChaCha's own headquarters—were there as well. The main members of the Valdez family were in attendance. One big happy family of like-minded individuals: all about getting money, loyal to each other, and lethal to all who opposed them.

Macho immediately saw his cousins: Javi, Xavier, and Evelyn. Javi was with his wife Michelle—formerly a contract killer turned family jeweler—and their two kids, Javi Jr. and Amara. Xavier was with his two baby mommas, Vanessa and their wild child Nena. With them were their children: Gianna, the daughter of Xavier and Vanessa, and Jordan, the son of Xavier and Nena. Jordan, at a year and a half, was six months older than one-year-old Gianna.

Evelyn was with her longtime girlfriend Gloria. Both Dominicans looked like thick-ass video vixens in tight sequined mini dresses, sexy designer stilettos, dripping in icy jewelry, with hair and makeup on point.

Beyond them, Macho saw his and Tool's grandparents, Juanito and Carolina, joined by the two brothers' great-uncle Diego, great-aunt Maritza, and their other great-aunt Larisa—the widow of the Valdez family's deceased king, Pedro. Larisa rarely left the D.R., so Macho could tell this wasn't a normal gathering.

The old heads of the family were worth billions each. Since the '70s, Pedro, Juanito, and Diego had been supplying the U.S. and Europe with grade-A Dominican cocaine, grown, cut, processed, and imported by their own methods—no middleman. They built an empire yet to be topped. But as life would have it, unavoidable tragedies hit the family, ultimately causing the old heads to pass the game to their sons. They suffered their own tragedies when Macho and Tool's father, Tomás, was killed. Avenged by Ricardo and Roselyn—parents of Javi, Xavier, and Evelyn—who had since gone into hiding in a faraway land to escape a certain federal death sentence due to the mass murder of federal agents they committed while taking out Tomás's killer.

The Valdez family business was handed to Danny, the youngest cousin of Tomás and Ricardo. He met his own drama when hauling a load of coke back from the East Coast. Illinois State Troopers caught up to him near Gurnee. He took them on a run and hit spike strips in the road, ending the miles-long chase. Danny ended up taking a hell of a long prison sentence, which shocked everybody, considering the protection left behind by the old heads to secure the future generations of the family.

Now, Danny's right hand, ChaCha, ran the show—and did so with an iron fist. She was loved and adored by the family, had been since she was first taken under Danny's wing at 18 years of age.

Macho held his woman's hand, and still, G-Baby's, as he headed to where his grandparents were. His brother and Tamilita followed, the crowd of people parting for them like Moses and the Red Sea, allowing them direct access to the O.G.s.

"La bendición," Macho said to his fair-skinned 6'0" tall grandfather, and his camel-brown 5'8" grandmother, greeting them respectfully like he and his brother had been raised to do.

Tool did the same, the brothers dapping their grandpa up and hugging their grandmother.

"Cómo han estado?" their grandma asked them.

"We been good, pretty lady," Macho answered, with an arm over her shoulder. "Y tú?"

"Blessed, papa," Carolina replied with a cheerful smile.

She and Juanito acknowledged and embraced the ladies like they were family. Juanito then spoke to his grandsons, his deep, powerful voice heard by others surrounding them over the laid-back reggaeton music.

"Tenemos que hablar," he told them. "Vamos."

Macho glanced at his brother, then without a word more, they followed their grandfather toward the stairway that led to the private rooftop section.

YESSINIA

She watched her man and his brother leave with Juanito and wondered what was up. She knew something was wrong, by the look on the hard-faced Dominican's mug.

"No te preocupes, cariño," Carolina said to her, touching her shoulder. "Todo va estar bien."

Yessy nodded her head at the old woman telling her everything was going to be okay. What Yessy did know was that Juanito was furious about that pesky DEA agent bitch harassing his grandson, and when Juanito was pissed, people died.

Javi and his wife and kids walked up just then, greeting Yessy, G-Baby, and Tomalita. Javi, golden-brown with long braids, a razor-sharp beard and hairline, stood an athletic 5'11". With green eyes, the 27-year-old looked like he could be a miniature Macho, instead of his cousin.

Michelle, a 28-year-old Dominican belle, originally from Manhattan's Washington Heights, compared to her Waukegan, Illinois-born husband, stood 5'5" with so much body she could turn a mob of homosexual men straight. Her brown sugar skin was flawless like the diamonds in her custom-designed jewelry; her long silky hair was intricately braided, resembling how the famed singer Janelle Monáe wore hers.

In Michelle's arms was the just-under-two-year-old Amara, half-Dominican, half-Puerto Rican. Amara was adored beyond belief by Michelle, which initially shocked everyone, especially Javi. The little girl had not been brought into the world by Javi and Michelle, but by Javi and his former honey dip, Angela, who had mysteriously disappeared not long after giving birth to Amara. Michelle didn't care that she wasn't Amara's biological mother; she loved her to no end as if she had birthed her.

Javi Jr. was a mini version of his pops, with the top of his head neatly braided, while the sides were faded perfectly. The 2-year-old held his father's hand, and was rocking Balenciaga like Javi, while his baby sister and mother were in custom FeFe outfits.

Yessy's iPhone rang as Michelle handed her daughter to G-Baby. Pulling it out of her tote bag, she saw ChaCha was calling. A photo of the Amazon-tall butter pecan Colomborriquena appeared on the screen. She answered, plugging her free ear with a finger so she could hear through the music.

"Yo! We here at ya spot and you're not!" Yessy hollered. "Where you at, ChaCha?"

"Comin' up the elevator now," ChaCha told her. "Yessy...I am very sure that I'm gonna need you and Gabi for... Nena control."

"Huh?" Yessy said, eyebrows furrowing.

ChaCha explained.

"Oh... damn, Mena! You called us together for that? Yo, like, that's something that should've been... handled, without almost a hundred people!"

"Well, it's... um... supposed to be a b-day bash too," ChaCha told her. "See you in... three seconds."

The call ended. Right away, Yessy told G-Baby what ChaCha had said. G-Baby gasped in shock. Tomalita was confused as hell.

The elevator doors opened up. Yessy and G-Baby tried to hurry and look for Xavier's crazy Greek and Mexican baby mama but couldn't help but turn to look toward the elevator.

The music stopped, replaced by gasps of shock and surprise. Inside the elevator, the 6'0" tall Colombian-Puerto Rican Ximena, A.K.A.. ChaCha, more than petite but just under thick, with piercing Arctic blue eyes and red wine-dyed hair, wearing a tight leather shoulderless minidress that matched her hair, eyelids, lips, and her pricey Gianvito Rossi stilettos. She had on fancy pantyhose with rose patterns woven in, two diamond chains around her neck, a diamond Richard Mille on her wrist, and diamonds hanging from her ears, visible due to the sophisticated upswept hairdo she rocked. The Jackson Heights, Queens, New York 32-year-old was looking like the billionaire that she was, but despite her alluring beauty, the eyes of everyone in her bachelorette pad were not on her, but on the amazingly voluptuous fire engine red-haired woman in the elevator with her, who held the hand of a young little girl, and was holding an even younger girl in her free arm.

"Bitch!"

Yessy heard Nena scream, and frantically looked around to find her, but the high yellow-complexioned mother of one was already sprinting in her stilettos toward the elevator, with fire in her eyes, and hatred in her heart, for the Cuban-American chick that had stolen her man, then, after making Xavier fall hard for her and her then-5-year-old daughter, the redhead up and vanished, leaving Xavier brokenhearted.

"Nena! Stop!" someone yelled out.

But she ignored them. Like a trained pit bull, she was locked on her Justin Valentine clone target, ready to go toe to toe for the umpteenth time.

Yessy and G-Baby were about to go stop Nena, when suddenly, she was scooped right off her feet by Tank, a massive 6'9"-inch-tall Samoan, pushing 400 lbs, part of Javi's crew.

"Tank! Let me goooo! Get ooofff!" Nena screamed, legs kicking, arms flailing as the giant carried her toward the outdoor rooftop terrace.

Relieved that they didn't have to put Nena in body locks, Yessy and G-Baby saw Michelle, Evelyn, and Gloria rushing off to lend Tank a hand, which he was most definitely going to need.

Yessy looked back toward the elevator, just as ChaCha led the three off of it. All eyes were on them, and that included the bulky 6'3"-inch-tall cocoa-brown Xavier, formerly the Dominican playboy of the Valdez family. He was staring at the redhead as if he had seen a ghost.

MACHO

"Lo sé, Grandpa," Macho said. "The bitch is just..." he quickly paused seeing the disapproving look on his grandfather's face. "I mean... ol' girl... she's just bored, man. Ain't nobody worried about her."

Juanito glanced over at his oldest grandson. Tool just shook his head.

"Nieto, tienes que usar la cabeza," Juanito said, and tapped on Macho's forehead for emphasis. "She is la policía; she can ruin you. Stop toying with her, Antonio."

Macho nodded his head. He stayed quiet, so as not to be argumentative with his grandpa.

"Ahora dime qué paso con esta situación con este personaje Pancho, and what has been found out about our coca being laced with fentanyl?"

Macho ran down the situation with the Ecuadorian drug dealer that had gotten involved in sex trafficking underaged girls, one of whom happened to be the young cousin of one of Macho's drivers. Juanito chuckled when Macho told him how it all went down—from faking Pancho out like he was getting his half-million-dollar re-up on coke, to finding the group of young Nigerian girls chained up in a subterranean level in his scrapyard office building. Juanito laughed his ass off when Macho told him about how Yessy shot Pancho in his ass crack multiple times with a nail gun, then about how

Pancho was sent to meet the family's most ruthless killer... Heavy B.

Macho then told his grandfather about El Demonio.

"That is who shot you, you are thinking?" Juanito asked, angry as hell to have almost lost his youngest grandson.

"He said to me, that he heard I've been looking for him. That would be my guess, and he been sendin' me text message gangsta shit, too." Macho handed his ol' head his phone so he and Tool could check the beef out.

"Bro," said Tool, speaking for the first time, always the one to think an entire situation through before giving his input. "I'm sure someone pointed this out to you, like ya lady or Gabi, but whoever this Demon clown is, he most definitely knows you. And I mean personally. Who you recently had beef with?"

"Pancho," Macho said, stating the obvious.

"Well, until this is figured out, you, Yessy, and G-Baby should go somewhere for a while, yo."

"Nigga, Javi and Michelle went through the same thing wit' that Victor Gomez clown, bro," Macho reminded Tool.

"Cabrón, that was different! They knew who was at them and knew how to get at him," Tool reminded Macho.

"Okay, okay, relax," Juanito said to them. "Antonio, your abuelita y yo feel it's—"

His words were halted when they started hearing yelling and screaming. They ran from the private terrace, back down to the main level, just in time to see Nena being carried away by Tank, kicking, screaming, and cursing.

With furrowed eyebrows, Macho turned his head and saw ChaCha coming out of the elevator, leading a woman that he thought he would never see again.

"Hoooooly shit," he said. "That's... Kenzie."

"And Nevaeh," Juanito added, speaking of Kenzie's 6-year-old daughter.

"And... another baby," came Tool, noticing how much more brown-skinned the child in Kenzie's arms was.

The 5'10" tall woman had milky white skin, and long, fiery red hair. Though she looked like a spitting image of the comedic TV show rap chick well-known for spitting bars on Nick Cannon's *Wild 'n Out*, embarrassing anyone that tried her.

Two years ago, after Xavier rescued her and Nevaeh from Kenzie's crazy and very abusive baby daddy and fell so deep in love with her, Kenzie had disappeared, taking her daughter and vanishing without a trace... until now.

Dressed in a red Valentino long-sleeved dress, matching pumps, hair and makeup did up, with gold jewelry, Kenzie looked so divine, that her ex-boyfriend wanted to run to her and kiss her instead of turning his back to her, the way she had done to him.

"Are y'all thinking what I'm thinking?" Macho asked as ChaCha led Kenzie and her kids up to a shocked Xavier, who was still joined by his daughter's voluptuous Puerto-Persian mother, A.K.A.., ChaCha's younger cousin Vanessa.

Yessy, G-Baby, and Tamalita came up just then and joined in on the speculation. Everyone watched as Kenzie, with tears in her eyes, handed Xavier the baby.

"Whoa... that's crazy," G-Baby said.

"She left him heartbroken while she was pregnant," Yessy said, speaking what everyone was thinking.

"Xavier needs to use condoms," Juanito said as his wife came to his side.

They all started laughing at the old heads.

G-BABY

"Mmmmmm, yeeeaaah! Ay papi! Yes! Dios mio, me encanta!"

She bit her lip as she arched her back. His face was between her legs, lips and tongue working her so good that she swore her head was going to explode.

On her back, ass naked, with white spike-toed red bottoms on her feet, G-Baby enjoyed the blissful sensation of the oral pleasure El Tiguere was giving her. She was going crazy!

"JUICY" by Pretty Ricky featuring Static Major crooned from somewhere. She could see nothing but the top of his head, and his hands keeping her legs parted while he dined on her love box.

"Shit, papi! That feels so good! God, I've been wanting this for so fucking long!" she told him.

He paused and lifted his face up from her wetness. The blue-gray eyes that had long ago cast a spell of love and desire on her made her reach down to pull him up on top of her.

His rock-hard, muscular, tattooed body laid on her soft, thick, tattooed body. She raised her lips to him and kissed them, tasting her own juices on them. He stuck his tongue in her mouth and explored her, his bone-hard cock throbbing on her inner thigh.

She laid her head back on the pillow and pleaded for him to enter her. He smiled and did as she asked. He slid into her, going deep, stretching her near-virgin walls out. She hissed from the sting but welcomed the pain. Pain was love, and she was in it.

He made love to her. She felt it. He never took his eyes off hers as he grinded, slowly putting it on her, keeping his strokes long and powerful. He filled her up with love, passion, and ecstasy.

She started shaking as he brought her close to climaxing. He kept stroking, working it faster, feeling her tunnel contracting around him as she leaked more and more.

"Ooooo I'm gon' cum! Fuck!" she cried out.

He went faster, pushing her legs up so that her knees touched her breasts. She hooked her arms under her legs and held them up so he could pound her harder, faster. Just as she came within seconds of exploding, Sevyn Streeter's "IT WON'T STOP" featuring Chris Brown came on. Then G-Baby came so hard that her legs went numb.

He roared like a lion, then busted his nut, cumming deep inside of her. He stayed inside her as he looked down into her eyes.

She looked up into his and could feel that he loved her the way that she loved him.

"I love you, too, Antonio! I love you so damn much, baby!"

His smile faded. "Gabi? Did you hear me? I said I love you, ma."

"Yes, baby! I love you, too!"

"Hey? Gabi?" He started shaking her. "Yo? Gabriela? Gabi!"

"Aya! G-Baby!"

She opened her eyes. He was here, at her side, shaking her. She saw Yessy at her other side, looking at her.

"Gabi? Wake ya' drunk ass up, biatch," said Yessy. "We home."

G-Baby then realized they were parked in front of her house.

Tool and Tamalita stood off to the side, watching as Macho and Yessy brought the Chicagorilla out of her drunken slumber.

"Whatever you was dreaming about had you moaning and squirming in the seat like someone was beating that cosita up real good," Yessy said with a goofy grin.

G-Baby sucked her teeth. "Naw, you tweakin," she capped, then grabbed her bag and got out of the car. "Deuces, shorties," she then said, hurrying off towards her built-in two-car garage, passing her wickedly fast SRT8 Jeep.

Macho, Yessy, Tool, and Tamalita watched as G-Baby entered a code, then the door raised, revealing a Lamborghini Aventador and her Bentley Flying Spur. G-Baby turned to them, hit a button to close the garage. Seconds later, she disappeared behind the garage door.

MACHO

The following morning, Macho found his woman in the kitchen, wearing a silk Versace robe, with her hair up in a messy bun. Shyne's old hit song, "BONNIE & SHYNE" with Barrington Levy bumped from the surround sound speakers in the sparkling marble and stainless chef-style kitchen.

Dreams got up from laying next to Maliante, who was sprawled out in the middle of the floor, and trotted up to Macho. He patted her head, then went to his sexy-at-all-times Nuyorican queen, wrapping his arms around her and hugging her from behind.

"Morning, beautiful," he whispered into her ear, planting a soft kiss on her neck.

She smiled. "Good morning, handsome. You hungry?"

"Starving, ya drained all my energy this morning, yo. What you looking at?" he asked as the song changed to Ja Rule and Ashanti's "ALWAYS ON TIME."

"I'm thinking... this," she said, making his eyes focus on the breakfast displayed on a page of her new cookbook.

"Oh snap! PB & J Cereal... French Toast?" he questioned.

Yessy showed him the cover of the recipe book. "Ayesha Curry's," she told him, as he saw the NBA star Steph Curry's wife on the cover, with Steph and their kids in the background, looking like a happy family.

"EEEEEEEE, I didn't know she had a cookbook out," Macho said.

Yessy showed him the front of the book, where Ayesha spoke of her multicultural family and the food she'd grown up on.

G-Baby entered the kitchen just then, wearing a tank top, a short leather Fendi skirt, and nude pumps. Her hair looked like she was fresh out of the shower. No jewelry, no makeup, just true beauty.

"What up, shorties?" she said, walking up to the dogs and crouching down to get a dog kiss from Dreams and Maliante.

"Shit. Bout to make breakfast. Wanna help?" Yessy asked.

"Sure."

Macho tried to keep his eyes off her, but as she walked off toward the pantry, he stole a glance at her phatty and almost bit his lip off.

G BABY

She grabbed a couple of cartons of eggs out of the fridge and turned to head back out to take them to Yessy, when her left heel slipped and she flew backward. She screamed as she went down, both cartons flying, smacking into the wall.

Dreams and Maliante ran in when they heard her. Macho and Yessy ran in after them.

"What the hell?" Yessy said, looking at her homegirl on the floor. "Still drunk?"

Macho laughed his ass off at her while the dogs sniffed and snorted at her.

"If you keep laughing instead of helping me up, I'ma beat cho' ass, Macho!" G-Baby told him.

He went and pulled her up as if she weighed nothing at all.

"Goddamn, Macho!" she said, as her breasts touched his sternum. "Yo strong ass, man!"

He laughed at her. "You aight?"

No! You're too fucking sexy! And I want some dick! But you're my best friend! And my best friend's man! Damn you!

G-Baby thought to herself, feeling her temperature rising from being so close to him.

"Uh huh. Yeah," G-Baby capped.

"Looks like the eggs didn't break." Yessy went and grabbed the cartons, opened them, and was amazed to see that none were broken. "Cool. Bring ya drunk booty on and help me cook, biatch," she told G-Baby.

Yessy exited the pantry, leaving the two alone with the dogs. Macho looked down at G-Baby. She avoided looking at him.

"For real. You cool, Gabi?" he asked again.

Her eyes went to his then.

No... I want to kiss you so badly, dude! Slip and fall on top of meeeee!

She nodded. "Yes. Peachy," she lied, then hurried to get away from him before she soaked through the little thang she had on under her mini skirt.

***

Forty-odd minutes later, Yessy and G-Baby had stacks of the peanut butter and jelly French toast made, fried up in sweet butter with flaky crushed Frosted Flakes like chicken in waffle batter, fried to golden perfection.

Fluffy scrambled cheese eggs, spiced with oregano, and caramelized apple slices completed the meal.

Tool and Tamalita joined them in the kitchen, just as they were setting the table.

Tool rocked a plain blue T-shirt that fit his massive upper body snugly, with Purple Label jeans and fresh white Air Forces. His dreads were loose of the 2-strand twists and hung crinkly down past his shoulders.

His woman, carrying their pup, wore a tight-fitting denim-topped skirt-hem dress. Her naturally curly hair was in a spiral fro. Down on her feet were denim wedge-heeled sneakers.

Angel got excited when she saw her father, wiggling and struggling to get free. Tamalita let her down and watched as she ran to Maliante, jumping on him while he lay on his side. Dreams stayed where she was, chilling close to the counter where the food was.

"What ya make for breakfast, mamas?" Tamalita asked in her Jamaican-sounding accent.

Yessy told her the name of the meal.

"Word?" Tool said. "That shit sound flame, and it smells so good!"

"We're gonna find out," Yessy said. "A woman with Jamaican, Chinese, Polish, and African-American in her gots to know how to cook."

Macho came back down just then, wearing a tank top, denim shorts, and Jordans on his feet. He dapped his brother and hugged Tamalita.

"Bro, lemme rap with you real quick," Tool told his brother.

Macho nodded, and the two headed out to the expansive backyard.

YESSINIA

"Ain't you curious about what they're talking about?" G-Baby asked Yessy.

"I know what they're talking about, Gabi. Tool's talking sense into Mr. Hard Head about that blank-ass mission that the fat dude's got Antonio going on."

"Blank mission?" Tamalita asked, hearing Yessy's words as she came back into the kitchen after feeding Macho's caimans.

"Yeah. Dude claims he needs Macho's help to pick up an old-school car for his grandma, coincidentally down in Texas, where all his family's dope comes from."

"Oh. No worries. Roberts will erase that idea from de man's head," Tamalita said, confident in Tool's ability to talk his wild-ass younger brother out of stupidity.

Just then, Yessy got a text notification. She saw the number on her iPhone screen belonged to Colonel Pane. Almost freezing in place, eyes wide, heart racing, she grabbed her phone and viewed the message:

Meet at TA Travel Plaza, Wadsworth area at 0500 hours.

"Yessy?" G-Baby said, puzzled. Her expression matched Tamalita's.

Yessy screamed, "Yes! Yes! Yes!" and then handed G-Baby her phone. G-Baby, too, went apeshit when she realized why their former Colonel was calling a meet.

Tamalita was beyond confused as to what had the two Puertorriqueñas so excited. Yessy and G-Baby explained to the Belizean what was up and the massive amounts of gwop that would come from such work.

"My God... de government will pay dat much for dat?"

"Tama, when you got the connection to make it happen, that's only a guesstimate," G-Baby said. "The government loves their toys and will pay an arm and a leg to get them moved around."

"We are more than happy to take a big-ass slice of that pie," Yessy added, then excitedly said, "Yooo, we about to really get this shmoney, son! It's on and poppin', yo! On God!"

"We about to get rich...er, biatch!" G-Baby threw in, and the three of them all screamed out excitedly at the chance to check tens of millions of dollars, doing something that Yessy and G-Baby did while in the Army, virtually for free.

Chapter 5

MACHO

While Tool shook his head, they both heard the ladies inside sounding geeked up about something.

"Ma ain't drop you on ya head when we was kids, so you must be shmoking something that ain't meant to be puffed on, Tonio. Are you hearing yourself right now?"

"Yep. I heard $15 million dollars for a two-day run. Did you hear it?" Macho asked his brother.

"I heard it, but what I'm not understanding is why you trying to help an op for chump change? Nigga, we got hundreds of millions just from when pops died and left us his bag, and that don't include what we both individually built and got gwop off of, yo! Homiez, you actin' crazy right now, bro!"

"Narco is my nigga, Tool. He helped us out, whether you wanna admit it or not, and he actually helped get Kenzie and Neveah's problem solved for real! There is nothing that's gon' stop me from making the trip. If you tryna box, then let's get to it, but swelled up or not, when he sends word, I'm out."

Macho prepared himself for the possibility of having to fight his brother. In no way was he scared, but Tool was skilled in many different styles of combat. Plus, he was huge.

Tool shook his head again. He looked at his brother for a minute, then spoke.

"I'm going with you, yo."

"Bro, you ain't gotta—"

"I said I'm going with you, nigga! Period! You buggin' hard with this shit, bro! We need to be findin' the nigga that shot you, and then replenishing all our people's yayo since the poisoned coke is gone!"

"We can get on that now, bro. We got time to shoot east. Have ya people get us a truckload ready."

Tool nodded his head. "It's already done. But yo, this business with fat boy, bro... this is *thee* last time! Homiez!"

Macho gave him an incredulous look. "Bro, how you gon'—"

"Last fuckin' time! On the homiez, yo!"

Tool shouted, cutting him off.

"Aight, man! Damn! Fuck is you yellin' for?"

Tool looked at his baby brother. He was beyond heated with Macho and his bullheadedness.

"Because, Tonio," he spoke. "You steady knockin' at the devil's door... one day, he gon' answer."

***

During breakfast, Yessy brought up a suggestion to Macho that he felt was actually a great idea. He went into his contacts, found Xavier's name, and texted him. Yessy's idea. A few seconds later, Xavier called.

"Dime," Macho answered, putting it on speaker phone.

"I'll ask her," Xavier said, his deep voice coming through clearly.

"Please do, cuzzo," Yessy chimed in. "I know she was struggling before she left. Gabi and I can help."

"I got it. Y'all good?"

"We straight. Where you at?" asked Macho.

"On the way down to Texas."

"Big oil field work?" asked Macho.

"You know it. Me, Good, Pete, Jeezy, and Thrax ridin' down to Kermit, with rock trucks for a sandmine company."

"Aye. If you ask nicely, Yessy might cut you in on this D.O.D. contract that she and our Gangsta Boo about to get."

"Yeah? D.O.D., though?"

"Yes, sir!" G-Baby jumped in. "Government money is guaranteed money."

"May I get in on it?" Xavier asked.

"Of course!" Yessy replied. "Since you asked so nicely and you have such cute little babies."

Xavier chuckled. "Thanks, future cousin-in-law. Email me whatever I need, and a schedule."

"Will do," Yessy said, liking the sound of what Xavier called her.

Macho ended the call. They finished breakfast, then he did the dishes while Yessy, Tamalita, and Tool went to go put on workout clothes. G-Baby sat at the island, trying to focus on something else, rather than Macho's bulky, tattooed arms.

He felt her eyes on him. He looked at her.

"What's wrong?" he asked, seeing something in her eyes.

She shook her head. "Antonio... please... I'm begging you… don't make that run for Narco. He is not your friend, man."

Macho stopped what he was doing. "Gabi. You know me. I'm a soldier. I don't run from nothin'. I run to what needs done. You, Yessy, Tool, ChaCha—y'all think he a snake, but he is the reason I'm alive right now."

G-Baby was astonished that he really felt like that. That he wasn't trying to acknowledge that Narco was the reason his life had been in danger. Taking Macho to rob him. They failed, but afterward, at a gas station, cops pulled up on Narco's car. Macho was driving. The gun was under his seat. Cops found it, and with his refusal to give Narco up—who had seen the cops at his car and ran, leaving Macho in possession of a hot gun—

Everybody was pissed at Macho, though could do nothing but respect his level of loyalty. As for Narco... he was dead to them all. The first chance anyone got to get him out of the way…

***

After a strenuous post-breakfast workout, plans were made to head east to New Jersey, where Tool's city-sized fuel and oil refinery worked 24 hours a day, producing fuels, oils, lubricants, and liquifying large amounts of cocaine fresh in from the Dominican Republic, via the Jersey docks.

Macho was gathering clean clothes to put on when he got a call from Narco. He immediately looked around the bedroom for Yessy. He heard the shower running and Reggaeton bumping.

"Yo?" he answered when he realized he had privacy.

"Bro, I got eyes on the bitches that was doin' that to yo' people's merch!" Narco said urgently.

"Who?"

"Tha nigga Julio, dog!"

"He's El Demonio? He isn't even a King! He a MP!" Macho thought out loud, thinking back to what Pancho had said.

"Man, I'm tryna tell you it's him, bro. I got all my lil' niggas on the bidness since you sent me details, especially when all them clowns you holla'd at said dude from Milwaukee. What chu' tryna do, bro? Talk more, or get on it? We out here posted and ready to have yo' back."

"My lady's gonna go nuts on me, man," Macho knew.

"You telling me your lady trumps the empire your family built off hard work, nigga? Come on, dog! You know for a fact that no matter what you do, she'll never leave you."

"Aight. I'm on the way," Macho said, then ended the call.

As fast as he could, he got dressed in black Dickies, threw on black Nike Air Force 1 steel-toe boots, and grabbed his all-black Pittsburgh fitted. He snatched the key to the monster he kept stashed in the garage of another crib and snuck out of the house with murder on his mind.

YESSINIA

"Antonio? Bae, can you tell the girls to be at the garage?"

Lathering up in the shower, Yessy heard nothing but water and the sound of Ivy Queen's "I DO."

"Bae!" she shouted.

Still no answer.

She groaned and got out of the shower. Grabbing her phone off the double vanity sink, she sent a group text to all the Numero Uno drivers to meet at the garage in an hour. Replies came in almost instantly.

"Antonio?" Yessy called out again, wondering why he wasn't answering.

Wrapping a towel around herself, she stepped out of the room. The dogs jumped off the bed and followed her. Just as she crossed into the hallway, she heard the roar of a monstrous supercharged LS9 engine.

Recognizing the sound instantly, she darted into the guest bedroom to her right and yanked back the curtain just in time to see Macho's pearl-black 1996 Chevy Impala SS bubble racing up Green Bay Road, heading north.

She gasped as it blew past the back of their house. Her heart dropped.

She ran to grab her phone and called him.

Straight to voicemail.

"Goddammit!" Yessy cursed. She tried again.

Same thing. Twice more. No answer.

"Tooool!" Yessy screamed, bolting out of her room in panic. She knew, deep down, that her man had rushed off to dive into something wild again.

G-BABY

She heard Yessy calling for Tool as she pulled on a pair of leggings. Panic laced Yessy's voice. G-Baby threw on a shirt, grabbed the Sig Sauer XM17 from under her pillow, and bolted from her room.

She skidded to a stop on the carpet when she saw Yessy telling Tool that Macho had just sped off in his Impala, without a single word about where he was headed.

Tool pulled out his phone and put Macho on speaker. Yessy's eyes widened when she heard it ringing.

"Yo?"

G-Baby heard Yessy gasp.

Tool opened his mouth, but Yessy beat him to it.

"Antonio! Where are you going?"

"Why you calling me off Tool's phone?"

"Answer my question!"

"Ladies first."

G-Baby jumped in before Yessy snapped.

"Macho, what happened? You know what just dippin' off does to her."

"Yo, I'm making a quick run to Racine! Chill out."

He hung up.

"This nigga just hung up on me, though?" Yessy said, looking like horns were about to sprout from her head.

"Relax, Yessy," Tool said. "I know he be wildin', but you gotta stay focused on what's coming at five. Tonio will be back."

"You seem real confident about that, Tool," Yessy snapped, just as Tamalita emerged from their room.

"One thing I'm sure of is my lil' brother. His ass too wild to die, yo. On the Homiez, death fears him."

Yessy shook her head. Without another word, she stormed off to get dressed.

"Did I miss something?" Tamalita asked.

"Nothing you haven't seen before," G-Baby replied, hoping Tool's words proved true.

MACHO

One Hour Later...

Macho exited I-94 in Milwaukee and rolled into Narco's hood. After hopping off National, shooting up 12th, and making a left on Madison, he arrived.

Posted outside a corner store, Narco and his young homies stood hoodied up, eyeing anything that didn't look familiar. Ten deep, custom-painted cars and SUVs on big rims lined the block.

Narco, 5'10", hefty with long black hair and deep brown skin that hinted at strong Aztec warrior blood, walked up to Macho's SS. Macho rolled the tinted window down.

"Park. This muhfucka too nice to get all bloody, bro," Narco said with a serious look.

Macho nodded, pulled the Chevy into the driveway beside the corner house, and hopped out.

An old gray, windowless Chevy van pulled up. Two men sat up front. The rest jumped inside, ready to roll.

Macho was about to grab his H&K G36 from the hidden rack under his backseat when Narco stopped him.

"We got everything we need, bro. Keep them pretty toys clean for now and let's ride. Nadia's boyfriend gave us a forty-minute window."

"My lady gave me less. So let's go," Macho said.

They both hopped into the van. The sliding door slammed shut. The driver hit the gas, tires screeching as they peeled off.

Macho was shown a few choice weapons. One in particular made him smirk.

Chuckling, he picked it up and its attachments.

"Now this is gonna be interesting," he said to himself, ready for war with anyone associated with the so-called Demon.

Chapter 6

YESSINIA

She tried hard to shake the feeling, but Yessy couldn't stop thinking about how he just up and left. No warning. No explanation.

It gnawed at her.

She and Macho had been thick since their mid-teens. Even through his prison bid and her years in the military, they stayed close. But lately? Things felt different. Distant.

She hated it.

Joey Bada$$'s "DEVASTATED" knocked through the speaker system in the back of G-Baby's Hennessey Jeep, the bass jolting her from her thoughts.

They were coming down Green Bay Road, almost to Wadsworth. G-Baby pulled into the left lane and stopped as the light at the intersection turned red.

AZ's classic "SUGAR HILL" came on. Yessy nodded to the beat. Old-school Hip Hop and R&B from New York always hit different.

Screeching tires snapped both women to attention.

Instantly, their Glock .40s were in hand, pulled from their handbags.

An orange Lamborghini Huracán skidded to a stop on Yessy's side. The tint was too dark to see inside.

The engine revved.

Yessy glanced at G-Baby, then back—just as the window rolled down.

"This fuckin' bitch!" Yessy spat when she saw Nayeli's lumped-up face.

The Chicana gave a twisted smirk, then hurled an egg at Yessy. It splattered on the window and oozed down.

"What the fuck, Joe!" G-Baby barked.

Nayeli smashed the gas, swerving into traffic.

Yessy and G-Baby watched her nearly get T-boned by a Numero Uno truck rolling east toward the yard. The driver slammed the brakes and blasted the air horns as the baby Lambo zipped past.

"Te lo juro por Dios, I'ma put that bitch in a meat grinder one day and feed her to my dogs, yo," Yessy swore, just as the light turned green.

She kept watching the Lambo disappear, until she realized they weren't moving.

Yessy turned to G-Baby and found her best friend staring straight ahead, frozen, eyes locked on Nayeli's fading silhouette.

"Gabi?"

A car honked behind them.

"Gabriela? Hey!"

G-Baby blinked, snapped out of it, looked over at Yessy, and then stomped the gas. The Jeep fishtailed sideways onto Wadsworth Road.

Yessy burst out laughing.

There was never a dull moment with her Gangsta Boo.

Down in the yard, Yessy saw that everyone was there. The sparkling turquoise-painted International 9900i Eagle, pulling a matching RGN Lowboy trailer with four axles, had just pulled up to the garage's oil-changing bay door, parking nose-first.

The driver's door opened, and out stepped the tall and voluptuous Afro-Brit, dressed in a Numero Uno Transport work shirt, tight skinny-leg jeans, and wheat Timbs on her feet. Her long, neatly twisted dreadlocks were styled in two-strand twists pulled back into a ponytail. Her ebony skin reflected deep Nigerian roots.

Right behind her came her huge, fawn-furred Bullmastiff, trotting beside his human as she stepped over to join the fourteen other ladies—and the only two males, besides Macho—that drove for Numero Uno.

"Alo thea', mates! N'oice ta see yoo 'awl today! Awlmost had a little Brenda thea before the yah'd turn-in, but me mate Bruno and I are A-okay!" she said to Yessy and G-Baby as they walked up.

"God, I freaking love her accent, sis," G-Baby exclaimed. "She's like... Tiffany Haddish, with a British accent."

Yessy laughed. "Word, yo."

The Numero Uno Transport squad consisted of all ex-military personnel. Most had been truck drivers in Yessy's and G-Baby's units, while a few others had served in different states.

Anake was a gold-skinned Egyptian woman, born in Cairo but raised in Chicago. She was twenty-nine, stood 5'5", and had long ink-black hair with a petite, athletic build.

Simone was a robust woman with a blue-dyed pixie haircut and a youthful face. The twenty-seven-year-old was a lesbian and was often joked about being the truck-driving version of the rapper Dej Loaf.

Nya was a fair-skinned Moroccan woman with dark brown hair, standing 5'6" with a voluptuous build. She was also a lesbian and had spent many steamy nights with G-Baby. She was twenty-nine, soon to be thirty.

Lauren was half Puerto Rican, half Mexican, born and raised in Waukegan. She was caramel-brown, with dark brown hair braided in eight neat cornrows. She was of average height and petite. At twenty-four, Lauren was the youngest of them all, but far from being considered a shortie.

DeeDee was brown like a milk-chocolate Hershey's Kiss. Her braided hair was wrapped and coiled on top of her head. The twenty-eight-year-old stood a statuesque 6'0" and was a head-busting goonstress. Ten solid years in the military had turned her into a tamed beast.

Shane and Mane were identical twins. They stood 6'1", with long braids the color of coffee with cream and sugar, and brawny builds. Shane was older by two hours. They were both approaching their thirtieth birthdays.

The Afro-Brit, Chloe, was the oldest of the squad at thirty-two. She was 5'10" of ex-British military might, born in Nigeria but raised in England before migrating to the States at twenty-six and becoming a U.S. citizen years later.

Brittany, a super light-skinned stallion, had long hair dyed a rich auburn color. She had the face of a model and the body of a dancer. She stood 5'7" and had joined the military at eighteen, discharging five years later. She'd been driving for Numero Uno for the last three.

Stella and Bella were identical twins from Manila. They came to the U.S. as children and gained citizenship after five years in Chicago. Now twenty-eight, the fair-skinned Filipino women had six years of military experience and two more driving for Numero Uno.

Maria and her cousin, Tatianna, were Dominican women from Chicago but raised in the northern suburbs. Maria, dark and lovely, was two years older than the twenty-five-year-old Tati. Both had five years of military service behind them.

Analise was a dark-chocolate Panamanian belle with her hair twisted into locks. She was 5'6", with wide hips, full breasts, and a big, phat ass. She had been a hit in her unit while stationed at Georgia's Fort Benning.

Tiffany was a redbone from Joliet. Her chestnut-colored hair was braided in an intricate design that made her look more runway than highway. A feisty 5'4" woman of twenty-seven, she was always down to ride for her Numero Uno family.

Perla was Venezuelan, raised in Chicago's Back of the Yards neighborhood. Loyalty and fearlessness were embedded in her. She stood 6'8", was thick, with rich caramel-brown skin and long violet-dyed hair. She was twenty-six and had been a truck driver for more than five years after two and a half years in the military.

Lastly was Victoria, half Cuban, half Puerto Rican. She stood 5'6", with golden dreadlocks that complemented her flawless cappuccino-toned skin. Stacked like a dancer and bad as hell, the twenty-nine-year-old had six years in the military and five more as a trucker, until a call from her former captain Medina got her to switch from TMC Transport to Numero Uno.

All seventeen squad members were lined up as if reporting for roll call. Yessy and G-Baby looked at them proudly and appreciatively.

Yessy explained what was coming and what was needed. After the briefing, they were dismissed with excitement over the new contract work. Everyone headed off to get their trucks and trailers serviced and cleaned in preparation for what felt like an imminent pop-up inspection.

Romeo pulled into the yard in his '97 S500 Benz and parked beside Analise's Audi truck. He hopped out, dressed to match the crew in a Numero Uno work shirt, cargo shorts, and Nike ACG boots. His long single braids were frizzy and needed redoing, but his low-trimmed beard was sharply lined—just like his baby hairline.

"Reporting for duty, Lieutenant Gina Rodriguez," Romeo said with a goofy grin to his sister.

G-Baby laughed at Yessy's frown. Everyone swore the bad Rican resembled the famous actress, but Yessy always denied it.

Yessy looked at G-Baby. "Something funny, Eva Benitez?" she said, noting how much G-Baby resembled April Hernandez.

"Dude, who the fuck is that, man? Macho called me that a while back."

"Watch *Freedom Writers* and find out, biatch," Yessy told her. "Anyways!" she continued, turning back to her brother. "You ready to join the big leagues, lil' dude?"

"Nigga, ain't shit little about me."

Yessy narrowed her eyes at him.

"Yes! I'm ready!" he said, changing his tone completely.

"Good! Go to the spare Eagle," she told him, pointing to a plain white 2004 International 9400 Eagle. "It's both a spare and a trainer truck for new hires. Get it ready for a pre-trip inspection, then hook up to the step-deck trailer next to it and pre-trip that too."

Romeo nodded. She told him where the keys were and sent him off. Her plans to train him and have him driving by the beginning of next month would add another driver to the company. She and G-Baby were still hoping two more would call soon, after they'd reached out.

"You think DBoy and Esmeralda just don't wanna drive anymore?" G-Baby asked, scanning the yard.

"Not at all. Truckin' is a way of life, not just a job. They'll call. I bet my life on it," Yessy said.

"Aye! Hold up, bro! Look!" said Pepe to his four homies—Chaparro, Zapata, Cuchillo, and Capone. "That's them bitch-ass Two-Ones right there!"

Strolling along Greenfield on the way back to Cuchillo's crib with packs of Swishers and beer they'd all chipped in for, Pepe—being the oldest—spotted a car that belonged to a rival mob he hated.

"Get they asses!" Zapata shouted, reaching under his navy-blue T-shirt for his piece.

Chaparro and the others followed suit. The silver E-Class Mercedes came to a stop at a red light, half a block away. The five rushed toward it and raised their guns to shoot—when suddenly Chaparro's head snapped to the right.

Zapata was instantly drenched in his blood. The others gasped when they saw the tip of an arrow jutting from Chaparro's skull, brain matter clinging to the metal point.

"¡Que chin—" Cuchillo began to shout, but another arrow shot through his left eye, exiting through the back of his head.

His body dropped, along with the two twelve-packs of Coronas. The others panicked and took off running for their lives.

WHACK!

An arrow shot through the back of Zapata's head, poking through the center of his forehead. He fell face-first and bled out on the sidewalk.

Pepe and Capone frantically looked around, guns out, scared shitless. Cars that had been passing by when their comrades got laid out skidded out of control and crashed. Tires squealed as a traffic jam began to grow.

Pepe saw it first—then Capone. The E-Class was speeding toward them, two people hanging out of the passenger windows, pointing ARPs in their direction.

"Shit! Dip, dog!" Pepe shouted and let off three shots from his Glock 9 at the Benz.

Capone popped off twice at the car with his Glock. They took off running when the AR pistols started spitting at them.

The two young MPs ran toward 16th, hoping to get to their big homie's crib on Muskego. There, they had plenty of reinforcements and an arsenal of weapons at their disposal.

"Get 'em! Get 'em! Get 'em, nigga! Go!" shouted Blick, the driver of the Benz, to his Two-One brothers dumping at the two surviving MPs.

Trigger and Clip squeezed round after round at them but managed to avoid getting hit as they reached 16th.

Blick stayed on their asses, fishtailing left on 16th, thinking about the $25,000 reward for killing all five. He wasn't sure what they had done to deserve such a large hit, but he didn't care. He wanted the money—period.

BRRRRRR! BRRRRR!

BRRRRRR! BRRRRR!

"Yeah! Aye, I got that nigga, folks! Stop the car!" Trigger shouted.

Blick hit the brakes, and Trigger and Clip jumped out. Trigger ran up to the MP he had shot in the ass, while Clip kept running and shooting at the last one.

BRRRRRRRRRR!Trigger popped the MP up, putting all the shots in the man's face.

"Bitch-ass rat," he spat.

WHACK!

Blick, still sitting in the car, saw his guy get hit with an arrow in the center of his forehead.

"Oh shit! Trigger!" he panicked, as Trigger's body dropped dead.

Tap. Tap. Tap.

"Aye, Blick," he heard.

Slowly, he turned his head and saw Gigante there, pointing a Mossberg pump at him.

"King love, bitch-ass nigga," Gigante said and pulled the trigger.

Pepe ducked and dodged bullets left and right as he kept running for his life. They came fast and close—too close for him to shoot back.

He heard the unmistakable blast of a shotgun just as he saw Muskego ahead. His heart nearly leapt out of his throat with relief. He ran out into the street, with the MPs' underboss's house in sight.

Right as he got to the middle of the street, an old van came speeding from the left. He saw it and screamed—just a millisecond before it smacked into him hard, sending him flying through the air.

MACHO

"Daaamn!" Macho burst out laughing as he and Narco's guys watched the fifth and final MP land on the windshield of a car, crashing right through it.

Gigante ran up to the car, pointed the gauge, and blew the pump—making sure the MP was dead.

He ran back to the van as Goldie opened the door for him. He jumped in, and Thunder hit the gas, taking off again.

Holding the crossbow in his hands, Macho loaded another spear-tipped arrow. Next to him, Narco held his AK-47. The seven others—BK, Moreno, No Love, Bully, Randon, Ojos, and Angel—all clutched assault rifles, submachine guns, and shotguns.

“Next stop: Big Daddy Demon’s spot,” Narco said to Macho as Thunder turned onto Muskego, en route to finish the job before their window closed.

“Bro, you my nigga, but that sounded so very gay, yo,” Macho said to Narco.

The Kings burst out laughing. Narco twisted his lip up and waved it off. Macho chuckled to himself, then looked ahead, out of the windshield—just as he saw Thunder and BK both looking to their right at a house they were creeping past.

Chapter 7

YESSINIA

Anxiously, Yessy looked at the time and saw it was close to two o'clock. She still hadn't heard from Macho, nor had anyone else.

Tool and Tamalita had come to the garage. Tool had El Viejo's engine hood open and was giving the Ol' Man some routine maintenance, while Tamalita assisted, checking the tire pressure for all ten wheels.

G-Baby had gone out to the little standalone garage, where the six remaining Caterpillar construction machines sat, waiting for their next demolition job.

Yessy noticed Nya sneaking into the little garage a few minutes after G-Baby had gone in. Shaking her head at how neither of them were slick, Yessy grabbed her laptop from her desk, brought it over to the couch in the office, and logged into her and G-Baby's real estate company's website to check for any property inquiries.

G-BABY

"Mmmmm... yeeeaaah, Gabi... shit," moaned Nya, back arching off the bed in the spacious mid-roof-style sleeper berth of G-Baby's brand-new Kenworth W900L heavy-haul tractor—a custom-built rig designed by Tool, with Macho's help. It sat next to the newly finished Peterbilt 389 heavy-hauler.

Ass naked, the two ladies were relieving themselves of built-up sexual frustration. The custom sound system in G-

Baby's luxurious two-toned sleeper boomed Ludacris' "HOW LOW," fueling them to please each other until they couldn't move.

Face down between Nya's legs, slurping her juices, G-Baby's phat, round, bare ass was up in the air. She sucked Nya's clit the way she liked hers sucked. G-Baby went wild on her on-and-off-again lover. The blissful moans and cries escaping Nya's delicious lips made G-Baby's pussy drip down her inner thighs.

She slipped in two fingers and stroked Nya while eating her out. Nya started trembling, shaking as she got closer to climax.

Seconds later, Nya cried out G-Baby's name—then exploded, squirting all over G-Baby's face.

"Holy shit!" Nya said, stuck and unable to move after such an explosive orgasm.

G-Baby got up, face wet with pussy juice, a slick smile on her lips as she looked at the wild expression on Nya's face.

"Why do you do this to me, Gabi?" Nya asked, as tears suddenly welled up in her eyes.

"Do what?"

"You act like you don't know me for days... weeks... then you tell me to meet you here, and you eat my pussy 'til I cum! I'm human, Gabi! I have feelings! Stop playing with them!"

G-Baby's eyebrows shot up. "That's why. You be tweakin', shortie! We ain't together! It's sex—that's all! Why the fuck do bitches be getting so damn emotional about casual hookups, Joe?"

"Maybe to some bitches, they might not see them as just casual hookups!"

G-Baby shook her head. "I do not have time for this crybaby shit."

"Bet you got time for Macho, though, huh?"

G-Baby stopped reaching for her clothes and looked at Nya. She glanced at the Middle Eastern chick, who sat on the bed with a smug smirk on her face.

G-Baby walked up to her. "What did you just say?"

"I said, you got time for—aaaagghh!"

Nya's words were cut short when G-Baby grabbed her by the throat with one hand. She squeezed, choking Nya out. Gritting her teeth, she grabbed her with her left hand too. Nya instantly went wide-eyed as her air was cut off.

"Listen to me real good, bitch! If you ever in your motherfuckin' life come at me sideways again, I will take your lips and your tongue! Try me! You know what I've done to bitches for way less!"

Nya frantically nodded her head, desperate to breathe again. G-Baby released her grip and watched Nya take a huge breath to refill her lungs.

"I'm sorry, man! You ain't have to get so fuckin' emotional about it, Gabi!"

"Bitch, watch your mouth and I won't! Macho is like a brother to me, and Yessy is like my sister. How the fuck you gon' shoot words like that at me, though?"

"It... I just notice how... you look at him, Gabi. Like... you're in love."

"No! That's my nigga, Nya! I admire and respect him! Get off that dumb-ass shit, Joe! On God, don't ever say no shit like that again!"

"Okay! I'm sorry!"

G-Baby grabbed her clothes and hurried to get dressed. Before Nya even had her bra snapped back on, G-Baby was out of her truck, anxious to get far away from Nya and hoping to dive into a pool of ice-cold Antarctic waters to cool off.

Cristiane ran to the door to see who was banging on it like the cops. Hurrying in her fuzzy slippers, she started unlocking all the high-strength extra security locks her man had installed. Too many break-ins and raids had prompted him to add six more in addition to the two standard ones.

BAM! BAM! BAM!

"Hold the fuck on, goddammit!" she shouted as she reached the last lock.

She yanked the door open and saw her man's arch enemy standing there.

"Oh heeellll no! What the fuck?" Cristiane immediately raised her .38 snub-nose revolver, pointing it at the brazen Latin King. "Yo fake-ass got a death wish, huh?" she asked, thumbing back the hammer, teeth gritted.

He chuckled. "Naw, shortie. I love life too much to die."

Cristiane saw another man step into view. He was taller than the hefty brown-skinned Mexican. His hair was in braided tails hanging to his barrel chest. He was huge, like he'd been lifting weights all his life. Cristiane looked into his bluish-gray eyes and faltered.

He looked at her, a serious expression in his gaze.

"Good afternoon, ma'am. We'd like a word with your man. Can you tell him we're here, please?"

"J-J-Joker isn't here," she stammered.

"Joker? Naw, I need to holla at—"

SMACK!

Cristiane was so distracted by the unbelievably handsome guy that her focus slipped from her man's op. He smacked the gun out of her hand, then socked her in the jaw.

Her head snapped back and she hit the floor.

MACHO

"Well damn! Did you have to hit her that hard?" Macho asked, as Narco grabbed the little six-shooter and tucked it.

"Fuck this bitch! We on business, nigga!"

Macho turned and saw the others posted up around the van, looking eager to finish and bounce.

"Aye, who's Joker?"

"Man, his name is Demon, bro! Don't let this bitch fool you! Niggas change names to stay low n' shit!" Narco said. "Bring yo' ass on!"

BOCKA BOCKA BOCKA BOCKA BOCKA!

Shots suddenly rang out from inside the house. Macho and Narco ducked instinctively. They heard a scream by the street and looked up to see Bully take a shot to the chest.

"Fuckin' punk-ass flakes! Get the fuck from my pad, dog!"

BOCKA BOCKA BOCKA BOCKA BOCKA!

More shots came. Macho looked up just in time to see a tatted-up dude in beige Dickies shorts, Nikes, and a tank top, dumping at them with a Glock.

"I assume that's Demon?" he asked Narco.

"If dude has a bald head and a mafioso mustache, then yeah!"

Macho peeked again and saw the guy reloading. He instantly hopped up with one of Narco's AK-47s and started firing.

"AAHH!"

Two rounds blew the guy's leg clean off below the knee. Macho ran inside, kicked the gun out of his hand, and pointed the barrel of the chopper in his face.

"What the fuck, dog?" the man cried, bleeding out all over the floor. "Who are you?"

"I'm the nigga whose coke you been putting fentanyl in and sending down to Illinois, makin' the punk-ass DEA come around, bitch-ass nigga!"

The guy's eyebrows furrowed. "What are you talking about? I don't move blanco, foo! On Sur Trece—I sell meth!"

"Uh huh. I hear you, Demon, but it's too late to cap, bitch."

"Demon? My name is Joker, dog! Demon is a La—"

BRRRRRRRRRRR!

Macho jumped back, startled by the chopper fire. He looked down and saw the MP shredded. Turning around, he saw Narco holding the K, barrel still smoking.

"A lame. I figured that's what he was about to say," Narco told Macho. "Mission accomplished. You ready to go?"

Macho stared at him for a moment, shocked.

"Bro! Aye! Wake up! You ready? Or you tryna have a beer with dude and his bitch?"

Macho left where he stood. He looked Narco in the eyes as he passed, then glanced down at the girl. He saw her eyelids fluttering as she began regaining consciousness.

BRRRRRRR!

Chopper fire erupted from behind. Macho kept walking, not wanting to see the girl bleeding out on the porch.

"You cool, fam?" Thunder asked as Macho climbed in.

He saw Bully was okay—a bulletproof vest under his hoodie had stopped the slug.

"Take me to my whip, yo," Macho said.

Narco jumped inside the van and slammed the door shut.

"Let's go!" he demanded.

Thunder hit the gas and peeled off, as flames from the small fire Narco started began spreading, consuming any evidence of cold-blooded murder that could lead back to them.

"Aye, my nigga? For a muhfucka that just got his revenge, you sure look unsatisfied," Narco said, seeing a frown on Macho's face.

Macho shook his head. "I'm all good, yo. Good lookin' on the help too. I'll make sure I return the favor."

"Just be ready when I give you the word to shoot south and grab that for me, and we'll call it even," Narco said. "Plus the money I already paid you."

Macho nodded. "No doubt, yo. Homiez, I got you, bruh."

Chapter 8

YESSINIA

Just as Yessy, G-Baby, and Romeo were about to hop into G-Baby's SRT8 Jeep, the growl of Macho's Impala caught their attention. Yessy looked and saw it coming down the path to the yard. It rolled over to the office, bent around it, and disappeared from sight. A minute later, Macho came walking toward them.

Yessy scowled at him as he approached. Ignoring it, Macho kissed her forehead, then, without a word, got into the back. Yessy glanced at G-Baby and saw her shake her head. Saving it all for later, they got in, and G-Baby pulled off, heading to the meet spot Colonel Pane told them about.

Dressed in casual clothes, Colonel Pane stepped out of a government Chevy Tahoe with a leather briefcase. He shook hands with Yessy, G-Baby, Romeo, and the infamous Macho Valdez. Then they headed inside the TA.

"All righty then. Welcome aboard with the United States Department of Defense—Captain, Major, Mr. Valdez, and Mr. Moralez," the Colonel said after everything was finalized. "You've all got my number. Any trouble at all, give me a call."

Rendered speechless, they all nodded. Colonel Pane chuckled, knowing the number negotiated for Numero Uno's services had shocked them.

He took his leave and exited the building. Yessy looked down at the copy of the signed contract and read it again. For two years, Numero Uno Transport LLC would haul everything—clothing, food, building supplies, communications equipment, artillery, ammunition, explosives, and any vehicle big or small—to and from all bases, camps, seaports, airports, and train depots across the country. Total payout exceeded $30 million, with 10% paid upfront and disbursements made each time a load was delivered.

"We did it... we did it… holy shit, we did iiiiiiit!" Yessy shouted as it all sank in.

Still shocked speechless, G-Baby couldn't form words. Macho, no stranger to big money, was beyond pleased about his woman and G-Baby's success. Romeo was proud of his sis and the Chicagorilla. He knew that whatever they did, they put their all into it—for better or worse.

"Good job, amor," Macho said. "How about a few drinks to celebrate?"

"Flannagan's!" G-Baby shouted, feeling the need to cut loose.

"Flannagan's it is," Macho agreed, pulling his woman to him and kissing her cheek.

She looked up at him and smiled lovingly, but deep down inside, she wanted to strangle him for leaving to go do God knows what.

Heading back to the house with Romeo and the dogs, Macho, Yessy, and G-Baby got fresh for a bussin' night out. Close in size, Romeo got his pick from Macho's extensive collection of designer swag.

Calls went out for the family to join the celebration at the popular bar. Javi, Michelle, Vanessa, Neva, Evelyn, Gloria, and ChaCha were all down to party hard.

Yessy slid her voluptuous body into a super tight FeFe bodysuit, styled like the "Queen Bee" ensemble Lil' Kim wore in the old rap video *All About the Benjamins.* She wore see-through 6-inch pumps, her hair flat-ironed and hanging down. She flossed out in white gold jewelry embedded with black diamonds—black eyeshadow, glossy pearl black lipstick, and black painted nails completing the look.

Macho rocked a black Gucci tracksuit with silver Gucci symbols monogrammed all over and silver Gucci sneakers. His long white gold rope chain had a custom Peterbilt emblem charm, done up in clear and black diamonds, matching the Cartier on his wrist.

G-Baby wore a cosmic silver latex dress with matching heels and diamond jewelry, her lips painted red.

Romeo was swagged out in a Ferragamo fit, complete with lizard skin sneakers and Macho's white gold vintage Presidential Rolex.

From another one of their house's garages, Macho went and pulled out his Mansory-edition Rolls Royce, sitting on 24-inch rims. The silver and black two-toned paint job was accented by a stainless-steel engine hood, and the rims gleamed like they'd never seen a speck of dust. Next to it was a brand-new matte black Cadillac Escalade.

Digging into her Gucci bag, Yessy pulled out the key fob to the special-order Cadillac truck. As Macho hopped out of the Rolls to open her door, she turned and handed the key to her brother.

"Okay, then! I get to whip the Caddy to the spot?" Romeo asked, as Tool and Tamalita came out of Macho and Yessy's house, looking like two million dollars.

"It's yours, baby bro," Yessy told him.

His eyes went wide in shock. "What?"

"I'm givin' it to you, Romeo—as an incentive to get it together," his sister said. "Plus, that old-ass Benz ain't cutting it, yo."

"And there's plenty more to follow, youngster," Macho chimed in.

"You ain't know?" Yessy grinned at him, dying to see his reaction to the rest of the gifts.

"Damn, son... Yo, sis—thanks," Romeo said, hugging Yessy emphatically. "I love ya ass, yo."

"Love you too, big head. Come on and chauffeur your big sis in your new whip to the party."

They walked toward the garage, and Romeo helped his sister up into the truck, which sat on black 28-inch Forgiatos. Romeo started the powerful supercharged engine and felt the SUV shake. He grinned like a kid in a candy store.

Macho turned and saw G-Baby looking nervous, twiddling her fingers.

God, she is so fuckin' bad, yo. Homiez, he thought to himself, nearly getting lost in the vision.

Puerto Rican perfection.

"Ready, lil mama?" he asked, standing at the front passenger door.

She nodded, lost for words, unable to look at him. G-Baby got inside the Rolls, Tool and Tamalita in the back, Macho behind the wheel. Romeo pulled his new ride out of the garage with his big sis riding shotgun. Macho got goosebumps from the sound of the supercharged engine under the hood growling through the high-performance Borla exhaust pipes.

Putting it in drive, he pulled off behind the 'Lac truck, turning the music on. Meek Mill's "Young & Gettin' It" featuring Kirko Bangz started playing, and the three 12-inch W7s in the trunk came to life when the beat dropped.

The popular bar was jumping for a Sunday evening. The parking lot was nearly full. Old schools, new schools, big rims, little rims—ballers and bad bitches made their way into Flannagan's. It was in the Great Lakes area, popular among northeastern Lake County residents looking to unwind and have a ball.

Turning onto the small side street off Buckley Road, Macho stayed behind Romeo. To his right, he saw his cousin Javi and Michelle getting out of her new chrome-green Lamborghini Aventador LP750 Superveloce Roadster. Next to it, his cousin Evelyn hopped out of her monstrous mint-blue 1967 Pontiac GTO convertible, sitting pretty on chromed 24-inch Forgiatos. With the golden-brown and thick 5'7" Dominicana was her equal-in-height, milk chocolate-toned girlfriend, rocking a tight leather dress and heels, and the 5'6" Vanessa in a skintight forest green bodysuit with stilettos on her feet.

No sign of Xavier or Kenzie, which didn't surprise Macho.

They entered the lot and backed into paved spots next to Michelle's car. As Macho killed the engine, bright blue lights hit the lot. Everyone looked toward the entrance and saw a Grigio Telesto gray Pagani Huayra riding in on blood-red rims that matched its interior.

The driver, concealed behind 5% tints, began revving the huge Mercedes-Benz V12 engine, creating the most exotic harmony of cylinder music. The rear tires started spinning, smoke pouring out as the Huayra hit donuts in the middle of the lot. All eyes were on the $2.5 million hypercar.

"When she pulls up, yo," Macho said with a chuckle, "she pulls up. Homiez."

G-Baby watched as the driver's door opened. Chuckling to herself, she saw ChaCha behind the wheel, stunting hard and letting everyone know that the boss bitch was in the house.

The mini dress ChaCha wore looked like someone had smashed a mirror and glued the shards to her body. Her mirror-shiny stilettos showed off her French-pedicured toes. Her hair was intricately braided in fishbones. VVS diamonds sparkled in the choker around her neck, the Patek on her wrist, and the Cartiers on her fingers. Red lipstick, a little blush to enhance her skin tone, black eyeliner, and Saint Laurent perfume completed her look.

"Heeeey, people!" she shouted, pimp-walking her way over to the others. "Fuck y'all waitin' for? Let's turn uuup! Wooooo!"

"Turn up, turn up, turn uuuuup!" G-Baby shouted, hopping up and down with the ladies, all of them ready to go crazy.

"Are we not the luckiest dudes on Earth?" Javi asked, standing with Macho, Tool, and Romeo.

They watched their women start twerking in front of their vehicles, ignoring Evelyn, the Valdez princess.

"Yes, sir!" Macho agreed, checking out his woman's booty clap game—and G-Baby's.

Tool licked his lips as he watched his Belizean queen shake her 38-inch bubble, not caring one bit that her short pleated skirt had risen over her ass.

Romeo ignored his sister and looked at the others, completely stuck on G-Baby and ChaCha.

ROMEO

I need me a chick like one of them, yo. Real shit, he thought to himself—just as the sound of whistling and catcalls erupted from a group of guys hanging out near a row of donked-out old school Chevys.

"Aye, shorty in the see-through bodysuit! Come slide with a real goon, joe!" one shouted, hands raised in a cocky challenge.

Macho knew the guy was talking to Yessy. He chuckled—not even close to entertaining someone trying to push up on his chick.

"Chill, cuz," Javi said, knowing his livewire cousin all too well. "We here to celebrate, not assassinate."

Walking with the fellas behind the ladies, Romeo felt his phone vibrate in his pocket. He pulled it out and saw one of his other breezies had texted him:

What's up? You really ain't fuckin' with me no more, tho? It's been a week since I've seen or heard from you, Romeo!

He ignored the text, turned his phone off, and slid it back in his pocket.

At the entrance to the bar, they rolled in eleven deep. The security guards didn't even attempt to search them—they already knew who had just stepped inside.

The spot had four sections, each with its own bar and different types of music for people with specific vibes. Toward the back, there was an open area with a dance floor that connected to a room with mirror walls and ceiling.

They entered the newest section of Flannagan's, lined with tall chairs and tables, a long bar, and a dance floor big enough for the whole crew to get wild. The guys grabbed tables and got drink orders from the ladies.

At the bar, Macho ordered Yessy a *Sex on the Beach*, D'USSÉ for G-Baby, and a bottle of 1738 for himself. Javi got his wife a strong *Long Island Iced Tea*, and Patron for himself. Romeo stuck with Remy Martin. Tool got Rosé for himself and his lady. The rest of the ladies ordered strong, fruity-flavored drinks.

"How you feel about the new venture, cuzzo?" Javi asked, nodding to Migos' "*Bad and Boujee*" featuring Lil Uzi Vert.

Macho nodded along to the beat. "Honored. My lady and Gab extended our portfolio again. They go hard, tiguere."

"Yes indeed they do, family," Javi agreed, proud to see his big cuz being held down by real ones.

Drinks in hand, they turned up—sipping, gulping, kicking it hard, laughing, joking, vibing.

Yessy sat on her man's lap while ChaCha brought up a deal she'd scored with the Lake County school district. Macho agreed to take on the jobs, stacking three major contracts on top of Numero Uno's plate—each worth millions.

Yessy screamed excitedly when Cardi B's *"I Like It"* featuring Bad Bunny came on.

"¡Baila conmigo, Antonio!" she shouted, slurring a little.

"No," he said, tipsy.

"Fuck you mean 'no'?" she snapped, forehead pressed to his.

"Did I say no? I meant, let's go!"

Yessy giggled, jumped off his lap. "Gabi! ¡vamos! Bring ya booty with us!"

G-Baby's eyes widened. She was tipsy—feeling it and feeling him… *waaay* too much.

"Sis… I—"

"Come on!" Yessy grabbed her hand and Macho's, yanking them toward the dance floor.

Romeo sipped his Remy and watched as Javi took his wife's hand and followed, along with the two lesbian lovers. Tool and Tamalita trailed behind. ChaCha, her younger cousin, and Nena were left at the tables.

"¡Que se joda!" ChaCha said. "We ain't gotta be wifed up to go dance, girls! Let's go! Come on, Romeo Don't Dance!"

Vanessa and Nena busted out laughing at turnt-up ChaCha. Romeo hopped up and went with them, feeling the Remy hit harder now.

YESSINIA

She leaned over and made it clap to the crazy Dominican-Trinidadian rap chick's song. She *knew* his eyes were on her—dick likely throbbing in his pants. Glancing over at G-Baby, Yessy saw her standing still like a flower.

"¡Gabi! ¡Mueve ese culo, bitch!" Yessy hollered, now touching the ground with her palms and throwing it *all* up in the air, drawing stares from every guy on the floor—a few of them getting slapped by their own women trying to copy the Nuyorican goddess.

"Yessy! I can't twerk for your man!" G-Baby shouted, avoiding Macho's eyes.

Yessy stood upright. "You ain't twerking *for* him, sis! You twerking *with* me! Now come on!"

MACHO

Lord have mercy on my libido...

He was awestruck watching the two juicy booties bouncing in front of him. Nio Garcia's "*Te Boté*" with Casper Magico blared through the speakers—and four thick, juicy ass cheeks moved to the rhythm like magic.

Yessy backed her thang into his crotch and nearly set him on fire. He split his attention between her and G-Baby, who now danced slowly—sensually—like the beat itself was making love to her. He bit his lip, watching her body move, wanting to be the reason she looked that close to climaxing… in her panties… or G-string… or maybe down her thighs.

He hadn't even noticed Yessy stop twerking and stand up. She turned around just as he took his eyes off her.

She pulled him in and started kissing him hungrily. Lifting a leg, she wrapped it around him, her pussy throbbing—so wet it soaked through the lace fabric of her thong, dampening the crotch of her Bumble Bee bodysuit.

"Mmmm, papi... *yo te quiero ahora mismo*," she whispered into his ear, then flicked his earlobe with her tongue.

"*Entonces, vamos pa' la Ghost, fresca*," he whispered back, his husky, wanton tone giving Yessy goosebumps.

Macho scooped her up in his arms and took off with her, counting the seconds it would take to get her to his Rolls and *put it down.*

G-BABY

She watched her friends dip off to go do the nasty—wherever they were heading to do it. Sighing, she was about to leave the dance floor when she noticed ChaCha, Vanessa, and Nena dancing around Romeo. He was looking like *the man.*

Javi and Michelle were slow dancing to Ivy Queen's sensually sexy *"I Do,"* as were Tool and Tamalita.

G-Baby felt her eyes welling up, emotions mixing with the buzz in her head. She started toward the tables when someone caught her by the arm, stopping her.

She spun so fast on the guy that he ducked on instinct, thinking he was about to get rocked.

"Whoa, whoa, whoa! Aye, shortie, chill!" the Hispanic guy said to her, hands up in surrender. "My bad, joe!"

"Fuck is you touching me for?" she snapped.

"I was just tryna get a dance with you," he told her.

G-Baby looked at him. He was somewhat hefty, fair skinned with a short spikey mohawk. He rocked a Bulls throwback jersey, designer jeans and sneakers with jewelry that looked cheap. He was clean-cut but wasn't G-Baby's type. "Naw. I'm cool, fam," she said, and turned to leave.

He grabbed her hand again. "Come on, shortie, don't be like that!"

G-Baby immediately started seeing red. Turning back to him, she was seconds away from rocking his jaw when Tool, Tamalita, Romeo, ChaCha, Vanessa, Nena, Javi and Michelle stepped up behind her. They all glared at the man.

"I think she said naw, my man," said Tool, taking a step forward to him, dwarfing him. "You touch her again, then you and I will dance."

The guy cowered in fear of the giant dread-head. "M-My fault, bro…I'm good for it," he said, and started walking off. He stepped towards Nena to squeeze through her and Vanessa and dip.

CRACK!

Nena cocked back, reached up and splowed his jaw, ringing the bell. He stumbled backwards, rubbing his jaw. Nena smirked at him. "What, bitch?" she shouted as he grilled her. "I'll beat cho' bitchass you touch my family again, joe! On my momma!"

ChaCha walked up to the man, towering over him. "Now's a good time for you to leave, buddy."

He split without another thought. ChaCha turned back towards the others and smiled as the rest of the people on the dance floor got back to moving and grooving.

YESSINIA

Young Jeezy's "SUPAFREAK," featuring 2 Chainz, bumped from the speakers in the Ghost, trunk rattling from the woofers pounding. Ass-naked, Yessy cried out in bliss as she bounced up and down on her man's dick. Her succulent 36DD cups bounced in his face, his hands cupping, squeezing, and smacking her phat ass. She worked her pussy muscles, clenching his cock with her tight tunnel, adding to the sensation that had his balls tightening up.

"Shit!" Macho hollered out, loving how good she felt.

Yessy treated his dick like it was a pogo stick, never wanting to stop. Minutes later, she screamed out and exploded, cumming all over him. He came after her, planting his seed deep inside of her. She leaned forward and kissed him with a lot of tongue. He muscled her onto her ass and slid down until his face was between her legs. Macho ate her up until she came in his face, squirting all over it. Then, with his dick back hard from pleasing her, he pulled himself up, ready to get back up in it.

Suddenly, tapping on the window startled them both. Yessy shrieked. Macho covered her with his body. They both looked at the left window and saw a man with a mask on, pointing a pistol at the window.

BOC! BOC! BOC! BOC! BOC! BOC! BOC! BOC! BOC!

G-BABY

She washed her hands and shook them out. Looking in the mirror, G-Baby groaned at her reflection. "Why? Why can't I have love?" she asked herself. "Why am I pining after my best friend's man?"

The ladies room door opened up and in came three young women, looking like they were street walkers in their skimpy outfits.

"Guuuurl, that man is fine! Did you see his eyes? Ooo!" said a tall dark-skinned girl with her dreads wrapped up on top of her head, wearing a bra top, leather skirt and stiletto boots.

"Hell yeah! I needs me a man like that!" said a thick ass redbone with long rust-colored extension braids, wearing a stretch tube dress with high-heeled sandals on her feet.

"Can you imagine those sexy ass eyes looking up at you after he eat the kitty cat?" The third girl— Hershey's chocolate brown, heavy-set, wearing a dress that looked a few sizes too small— caught goosebumps. "I'll sit on his face and drown his swole ass, bitch. Then I'ma braid his hair and cook for him," she said.

G-Baby shook her head. She just knew they were talking about Macho.

"Um, 'scuse me? You got a problem?"

G-Baby saw the tall chick looking at her. The other two were as well. "Naw. No problem. I was just leavin," G-Baby said, stepping towards the door. "And FYI…he has a woman who you should not piss off by bumpin' y'all gums about him."

"Bitch, don't nobody give a fuck about his hoe!" the redbone snapped, stepping in front of G-Baby, blocking her exit. "Mind yo'muthafucking business!"

"Yeah, hoe!" the tall chick said, stepping up at G-Baby's left.

The heavy girl stood behind her, balling her fists up.

G-Baby looked at the red bone. "This is a warning…Move or I will hurt you all...really bad."

The tall girl cocked back and swung a hard right. G-Baby ducked a millisecond before the girl could connect. She thrusted herself backwards into the heavy girl with enough force to knock her on her ass. The redbone and tall girl ran up on G-Baby at the same time, swinging wildly. G-Baby faked left, psyching them out, then shot right. She pivoted hard and hit the redbone with a lightening fast 3-punch combo, sending her to the floor, K.O.'d. The tall girl saw her two friends on the floor and grew hesitant. The girl hadn't even taken her pumps off and had dogged her bitches out.

"Come on, hoe!" G-Baby dared her, gunned up and ready to thump.

"Hell no!" the tall chick panicked, then made a break for the door.

"Uh uh! Fuck you think you're goin', puta?" G-Baby said, jumping at the woman and grabbing her. G-Baby yanked her away from the door, then spun a powerful roundhouse kick, catching the girl in her jaw.

The girl flew sideways and landed on the heavy girl, dazed and seeing double of everything. G-Baby was about to kick the girl's jaw off when she started hearing screaming and shouting outside of the bathroom. Forgetting about the girls, she rushed out and saw females running in from the bar's entrance, looking terrified. Then, she heard gunshots coming from outside. G-Baby's heart dropped as her instincts screamed, *YESSY! MACHO!*

She ran as fast as her heels could carry her out of the bar. People were running, scattering, screaming for help. She looked towards where her people had parked and saw a darkly clothed figure shooting at Macho's Rolls-Royce. "MACHO! YESSY!" G-Baby screamed. Fearlessly, she took off running towards the shooter, her eyes locked onto him. She'd lost count of all the shots, focusing on getting to her homies.

The guy took off running after firing eight more shots. He got five steps away and was clotheslined by G-Baby. He flew backwards, gun flying out of his hand. G-Baby dropped down to him hard with her knee, cracking his ribs. He shouted in pain as she brought her knee down again, breaking a few more ribs. She made sure he was immobilized before getting up. She looked at the Rolls, no damage done to it at all. The invisible armoring that Macho dropped a bag to have put on the Ghost could stop everything up to 7.62-millimeter rounds...but not for too long.

Tool, ChaCha, Javi, Evelyn, Romeo, Nena, Vanessa, Michelle, and Gloria ran out just then and saw the shooter on the ground, screaming in agony.

"What the fuck, yo?" ChaCha asked in panic.

"HELP ME! PLEASE!" the shooter cried to her.

WHAM!

She delivered a field goal kick to his face, blacking him out.

Romeo ran to the rear door of the Rolls and called for his sister. "Yo! Sis! Sis!"

The window rolled down a few inches. "Um…we're fine," she said, "but...kind of naked…Can 'ya give us a second?"

Romeo shook his head and looked at the others as the window rolled back up.

MACHO

"Aaaghhh! Aaaghhh! Aaaaaaggghhh! Stooooooooop!"

"Tell me who sent ya' dumbass, and I will," Macho said, keeping his foot down on the man's broken ribs.

Having tossed the shooter in Evelyn's trunk, the Valdez clan got up out of the bar's lot before North Chicago police could make it there. They sped an hour north, hopping off of the interstate in Oak Creek, Wisconsin, and ended up in a secluded area along Lake Michigan.

"And if you lie again, I'ma cut cha' balls off and make you eat them!" Yessy threatened with a razor-sharp butterfly knife in her hand

Surrounding him were G-Baby, Tool, Tamalita, ChaCha, Evelyn, Gloria, Vanessa, Nena, Javi, Michelle, and Romeo— every single one of them with Glocks in their hands, cocked and ready.

"I-I-I was robbing you!" the man cried.

"Liar," Macho said, then told his woman to do her.

G-Baby and Romeo rushed in to assist, yanking the man's pants and boxers down, exposing his pecker.

"No! No! No! No! Nooooooo!"

Yessy grabbed the tip of his piece and sliced clean through the base.

"Aaaaaaahhhhhh fuuuuuuuuuck!"

ChaCha walked up and grabbed the man's face while G-Baby and Romeo assisted Macho holding the guy down. She stuck her hands in his mouth and forced it all the way open. Yessy stuffed his severed cock into his mouth and pushed it as far down his throat as she could.

He gagged on his dick, grasping at his throat when everyone let go. They watched as he suffocated to death. Taking his last breath, he went limp, dead eyes still open, staring up at the black sky.

Macho started singing out of nowhere as they stared at the dead shooter's corpse.

"Na na na na…na na na na…hey heey heeeey. You dies! Biiiiitch!"

Chapter 9

Early the next morning, Macho woke his woman up with a hot wake-up session. He put a bright smile on her face, then took her into the shower and loved her up against the wall until she drenched him like the rain-down shower head.

He washed her body, she washed his. They got out, dried each other off, lotioned up, then stepped into their walk-in closet to get dressed. They had a job to do—and they were both excited about seeing ol' Freddie Fred and Beautiful.

Macho pulled on his *Numero Uno Transport* work shirt, jeans, and Timberlands. Yessy wore a pearl-blue dress blouse, matching slacks, and flats, with her hair in a bun and no makeup.

Down in the kitchen, they were surprised to find G-Baby had made them breakfast sandwiches—fried ham, egg, and cheese on toasted croissants with tater tots on the side.

"Well damn, ma," Yessy said, hugging the work-ready Chicagorilla. "You came charging in to save our lives and cook breakfast?"

She almost blushed when Macho looked at her, awestruck by how truly gangsta she was.

"I love y'all," G-Baby said, simple as that. "And I don't mind showin' it."

"Aww! We love you too, crazy bitch!" Yessy said, wrapping her up in a bear hug.

G-Baby chuckled. "Me? Crazy? You just cut a nigga's dick off and made him choke to death on it."

"So? He lied."

"Nobody picks a Rolls-Royce to start dumpin' on the people inside, if they really tryna hit a lick," Macho said. "He had a tattoo of the Ecuador flag on his neck."

"Pancho's people?" G-Baby guessed.

"I'd bet on it. And I'ma find out who they are—real soon," Macho said, already knowing how quick his cousin Danny could dig people up.

"Until then, off to see Antonio get his ass kicked by his baby sister! Yaaaaay!" Yessy hollered, grinning at her man.

He waved her off. "Beautiful ain't no fighter, bae. She might be a lil' swol' at me for goin' ghost, but she always gets over it."

Yessy and G-Baby exchanged glances, then burst out laughing.

TOOL

Outside with Romeo, Tamalita, Angel, Maliante, and Dreams, Tool gave the young buck a quick CDL quiz to make sure he was sharp for the day.

After five perfect answers, Tool was confident. Romeo was ready.

Yessy and G-Baby came out the house with Romeo trailing behind. Tool nodded in approval. What he saw was a tight-knit trio with an unbreakable bond. He'd met very few people with that kind of loyalty.

Yessy pulled out in her S650 Maybach Benz. She took the wheel, Macho and Romeo in the back with the dogs, G-Baby riding shotgun. Tool, his lady, and their pup hopped in his Range and followed behind to the yard.

On the way, Tool got a call from Danny. The Ecuadorian shooter had been traced—addresses and numbers secured.

"Period," Tool said. "Good look, cutty."

"Yep," Danny replied, then hung up.

"When we gonna go get 'em, Roberto?" Tamalita asked, using his government name like always.

"Soon, baby. They expectin' retaliation. But we don't let 'em see us comin'. The element of surprise keeps goofies lookin' over their shoulders."

YESSINIA

"Aay, mira, Gabi! She's here!" Yessy said as she pulled into the *Numero Uno Transport* lot.

Among the seventeen drivers, a 6'1" American-born Syrian woman stood out. She wore a V-neck shirt, tight jeans, and work boots. Her long, ink-black hair hung just past her shoulders. Her skin was the color of vanilla wafers. She was athletic with wide hips, a round ass, strong legs, and a heart-shaped face that made it hard not to stare.

Esmeralda was just shy of 30.

G-Baby screamed excitedly when she saw her.

"Who's she?" Romeo asked.

"Esmeralda," Yessy said, parking her Maybach near the office. "One of the beasts in our unit. She's joining the team today. I was hoping DBoy would show up too… but he's dealing with some family shit."

They stepped out and got greeted by the drivers. Excited, Yessy and G-Baby introduced Esmeralda to Romeo and Macho.

Macho was taken aback. He'd never seen an ugly Middle Eastern woman—but Esmeralda was on another level. Indescribable. And her voice? Like a singer's.

"Heard about you, Romeo," she said.

"Yeah?" Romeo flashed a sly smile. "Heard how young, fresh, and fly the kid is?"

Yessy and G-Baby burst out laughing. In unison, they shouted, "Womp womp!"

Esmeralda giggled just as Romeo scowled at his sister, knowing she probably said something reckless that ruined his chances.

"Uh, more like you had a big head when you were born," Esmeralda said.

Yessy and G-Baby laughed harder. Romeo did not.

***

The *Numero Uno* crew was ready. Everyone was posted at their rigs—coupled to heavy-duty hydraulic-powered RGN lowboy trailers, with either three or four axles. They could all carry between 110,000 and 120,000 pounds.

Shane and Mane had their twin male Gotti-line steel blue and brindle pit bulls along for the ride. Shane's dog, Biggie, and Mane's, Boosie, loved the road life in their owners' big, tricked-out Peterbilt 379 Extended Hoods.

Stell and Bella stood proud in front of their custom-painted International HX rigs. Next to them were Chloe, her cousin Taranda, and Chloe's brute of a dog—posted up in front of Chloe's Eagle 9900i International hauler.

Tiffany stood at her heavy-spec'd Kenworth T800. Simone was in front of her Freightliner Classic XL, which wasn't a heavy hauler, but happened to be the first truck that Macho ever owned, and made millions off of.

DeeDee and her ocelot, Vera, were in front of her heavy hauler Peterbilt 389, next to Victoria, her female Razor's Edge bluenose Pit Bull, Kenya, and Victoria's Peterbilt 367 heavy haul tractor.

Anaka had her two French Bulldogs, twin brothers, ready to go for a ride in her non-heavy-spec'd Kenworth T660. Mari and Tatianna had their dogs as well. Maria's brown-and-white brindle puppy Bull Terrier sat obediently at her side, as did Snow and White, Tatianna's two all-white German Shepherd pups. Snow and White were anxious herself to take her recently bought International Eagle 9900i and get money alongside her cousin in her 9400i Eagle International.

Lauren and her heavy haul Kenworth T800 were ready to roll. Analise and Brittany, pushing a Peterbilt 389 and a

Kenworth W900L, stood with Perla and Nya, both by Perla's 367 Peterbilt and Nya's International Paystar 5900i.

YESSINIA

She kissed her man on his lips and held onto him for a minute. "I can't wait 'til this week is over. I'm ready to get on the road and ride with you legally, in my truck," she said.

"Me too, amor. Until then, we'll save the big loads for you," he replied.

Yessy got another kiss, then hopped into her Maybach to head to the base and get started on her week-long classes that she had to take to become a civilian again.

G-BABY

"Oh shit! Daaaaaamn, girl!" Esmeralda was shocked to see the Chicagorilla's ride after following her into the standalone 2-bay garage next to the main garage. "This how you doin' it, though? And Yessy, too?"

The custom-built Kenworth W900L was a special build, put together from the bare frame. Macho and Tool turned the reinforced frame into a one-of-a-kind W900L. Heavy-duty everything went into it. Then to complement the Crystal Ivory paint, a surplus of exterior chrome, wood, and leather. Behind the cab, the 70-inch-long flat top-style sleeper berth had been done up to match the luxury of a Rolls-Royce Phantom.

G-Baby's large car was built to haul some seriously heavy loads. With the brand-new quad-axle RGN coupled to it, the lowboy, painted to match the rig, had four axles with air-ride suspension, and had its own small gas-powered engine mounted in between the gooseneck-shaped hitch at the front of the RGN to power the lowboy's hydraulic system.

Next to the W900L was Yessy's big, bulky Peterbilt 389 heavy hauler. The sparkly Côte d'Azur blue paint job and the gleaming chrome gave Yessy's big rig such a majestic look, and its cab interior—and inside the 78-inch stand-up style sleeper berth—had custom touches that made Yessy feel like she was climbing up into a lavish Gulfstream jet. The 389 was also coupled to an RGN with four axles, allowing Yessy to carry loads that weighed up to 60 tons.

"You know how we do, Joe," G-Baby said to Esmeralda, feeling herself as she went to unlatch the long elegant engine hood's straps. "Hop up inside and put my log on 'Pre-Trip' for me," she then requested of the Syrian, to electronically display the time it took for G-Baby to perform the mandatory Pre-Trip inspection on her tractor and her trailer.

Esmeralda opened the driver's door and climbed up into the decked-out cab. It still had plastic on the seats and still had that new truck smell.

Seeing the Apple iPad connected to a charger cord, Esmeralda grabbed it and lit the screen up. She pressed the E-Log app icon, and when the duty status menu selections came up, she pressed 'On Duty/Not Driving: Pre-Trip,' starting the time for the inspection, which needed to be thoroughly performed to ensure the heavier-than-normal 30-wheeler semi was safe to drive.

MACHO

"Bro, this muhfucka is off the chain, yo!" Romeo said, admiring Macho's special Legacy Class edition 2007 Peterbilt 379 Extended Hood. It was candy-painted an exquisite Dark Jade green, chromed out to the max, the frame custom-stretched longer to give it that highly coveted hot rod truck look. The custom stainless front bumper kissed the ground from the custom Gen Z front axles air-ride suspension.

It looked angry. The chrome V-shaped windshield visor made the truck look highly upset, and the huge 10-inch diameter chromed exhaust stacks allowed for the insanely powerful Caterpillar engine under the long custom engine hood to roar while it breathed fire.

The Legacy Class was Macho's rolling work of art—but not because of the work he and his brother put into it to boost its value to $650,000. The Legacy's value was sentimental.

Before their mother succumbed to lung, liver, and kidney cancer, Macho and Tool took her all over the country on long hauls, giving her the best last few weeks of her life—before she joined their father up in forever paradise.

"Can I get one of these when I get my first truck?" Romeo asked.

"If you can find one," Macho replied, giving Dreams a belly rub. "Only 1,000 of the Legacies were made before the 378 was discontinued and the 388 took over, but later for the talking."

Macho stood and went to unlatch the engine hood on both sides, then, standing in front, he gently pulled the hood forward.

"Damn, yo." Romeo's eyes fixated on the clean yellow thing—turbocharged C15 engine, upgraded with high-performance diesel parts from Pittsburgh Power, Inc., one of the best truck engine modifying businesses on Earth. "This engine got as much chrome as the actual truck got."

Macho chuckled at the starry-eyed gaze on the young buck's face. When it came to big fancy trucks, Macho and his family did it up like rappers in diamond jewelry and designer swag. It was culture—and had been for as long as Macho had been alive.

Following his instructions, Romeo climbed up into the Dark Jade and black cab, sitting on the green and black alligator and ostrich-skin air-adjustable driver's seat. He grabbed the iPad charging up on the dashboard, turned it on, and went to the Trip Log app.

Macho explained the different duty statuses to Romeo, teaching him what to use for doing his pre-trip, stopping for fuel, a break, sleep, loading, and unloading. He taught him about *Personal Conveyance*, a status for drivers needing just a little more time to get to their destination, though their drive time had run out. He explained it all so that Romeo's logging would be correct whenever he hit the road on his own and pulled into a D.O.T. weigh station to get weighed. If a trucker's log was not correct, big fines and shut-downs would be the repercussions.

After Romeo checked the radiator for the coolant, the condition of the hoses from it to the engine, and the belts that spun the engine's fan, he checked the engine oil tank, the power steering fluid, and windshield wiper fluid. Macho made sure he checked over the steering system, then the front suspension and the axle. Once Romeo looked under the engine's oil pan, saw no fresh leaks of any kind, then down under where the 18-speed transmission was bottled up, under the cab, seeing no leaks there, he gave Macho a thumbs up.

"Aight. Close the hood, latch it up; climb up inside, and before you start the motor, make sure the shifter is in neutral, and push the clutch pedal in."

Romeo nodded and did as instructed. Macho heard the sounds of G-Baby's powerful X15 Cummins engine start up just then. A symphony created by her 1,000-horsepower diesel engine, and a 1,400-horsepower Caterpillar engine under the hood of an old '85 Pete 359, dubbed *El Viejo,* was damn near as enjoyable to hear as his woman crying out his name.

When his own 1,350-horsepower Cat started up, Macho got goosebumps. His rig was so loud that you'd have trouble hearing an AK-47 being fired right next to it.

Romeo looked down at the customized dashboard and watched the gauges. He knew the engine oil pressure and engine oil temperature should rise to normal in seconds. The voltmeter and coolant temperature gauges were working and rose to normal idling range. He looked at the air pressure gauge and saw the two needles inside rising as air pressure rose. The low air warning buzzer sounded off as air built up in the tank via air compressor under the hood. The low air warning light was on as well.

Romeo waited as the air pressure reached 60 psi. Once it surpassed 60, the buzzer cut off, but the warning light stayed on. He continued watching the steady rise as it went from 85 psi to 100 psi within forty-five seconds. The warning light then cut off.

"We good, bro," Romeo hollered down out of the open suicide-style door.

Macho nodded as he held Dreams's paws up while she stood on her hind legs.

"Do your walkaround now," Macho told him. "Check everything. We don't support cutting corners."

Romeo got out to do his walkaround inspection once he turned on the exterior lights. Just then, Macho heard trucks entering the yard before he saw them. The 2006 X-Edition Peterbilt 379 Extended Hood, painted in Ferrari Rosso Corsa Red paint, chromed out to the max with big 10-inch Dynaflex exhaust stacks, amplified the monstrous engine's roar as the driver hit the jake brake to slow the decked-out rig and its step deck trailer to a stop by where Yessy and G-Baby's private parking garage was.

Behind it, a 1984 GMC 5-Star General, looking as shiny as it did when it came out the manufacturing plant. Silver metallic paint with blue pinstriping, shined-up stainless steel exterior parts and 7-inch straight stacks, pulling a step deck trailer as well.

Macho smiled seeing the two rigs. ChaCha got out of the X-Edition in a denim bodysuit, Timberlands, with a New York fitted on her cornrowed head. Behind her, Pablo, her massive brindle Presa Canario that looked like a tiger-striped Great Dane with a Pit Bull's head. Pablo was a monster-sized Mastiff, his ancestry originally created in the Canary Islands. He was fiercely protective of his human, highly trained to immobilize and kill with little effort at just two years old.

"What the fuck? Yo, Pablo look like a damn tiger, son!" Romeo said, looking at ChaCha's demon dog as he stuck his huge head out of her window.

The General parked behind ChaCha's X-Edition. Macho saw his grandfather get out from behind the wheel of the vintage rig, catching a glimpse of his grandmother's tiger-brindle English Bulldog, Santo.

From around the driver's side came Carolina, walking with her husband, taking his hand with hers that had the 9.5-carat blue diamond wedding ring that Juanito spent $20 million on back when he proposed to her nearly half a century ago. ChaCha walked with them as they headed in Macho and Romeo's direction.

"Now it's a party," Macho said, geeked to have those that came before him along for the big job.

Chapter 10

YESSINIA

Stopping at a gas station to fill her Maybach up with premium, Yessy nodded her head to Nengo Flow's *"TARDE O TEMPRANO,"* with Miky Woodz and Lito Kirino on the track. Leaned up against her car, she waited for her tank to fill.

A text message came to her iPhone just then. Seeing the screen light up, she grabbed it off of the center console and saw it was a picture message. Opening it, she gasped.

"Awww! My baby as a baby!" she cooed, looking at the picture of a very young, light golden-brown, blue-eyed nappy head. "Antonio, you were so damn adorable as a baby."

Yessy then noticed that the photo came from a random number. Furrowing her eyebrows, she looked at the number, not recognizing it. It had an 847 area code, signifying that it had come from a phone registered in Lake County, but the last seven digits were foreign.

She texted, "Who is this?" to it but got no reply. She then called it and got no answer. Shrugging it off, she decided to forward it to Macho, adding a caption saying, "Cutest Yellow Boy Ever!!!"

The gas pump nozzle clicked when her tank was full. Yessy capped the tank's spout, hopped back inside, and started the powerful twin-turbo Brabus V12, pulling off, anxious to get her first day of class done and over with and get back to her family.

MACHO

This is not me... sorry.

Macho sent the text to his woman when he saw the picture of the kid she sent him. Romeo called to him, letting him know that the 5.3-foot-long step decker trailer Macho had pulled the Legacy Class out of the garage and backed to was coupled up and ready to roll. Tool had pulled *El Viejo* out of the bay and got coupled to another step decker trailer.

Climbing up into the Legacy's cab with the dogs and Romeo, Macho grabbed the iPad and put his duty status onto "Driving," starting his drive time. Since he was pulling a trailer, he was limited to driving for just up to eleven hours. If another licensed driver was pulling with him, they could alternate and keep the wheels turning, bank account earning. When one ran out of time, the other took over while the first driver took their ten off. They switched when one couldn't drive any longer and continued taking turns.

For drivers getting paid by the mile, a truck that never stopped moving, never stopped making money. Team truckers could earn $200,000 a year and more, but not everyone was capable of being in a truck with another person for days, weeks, and/or months at a time.

Macho led the way out of the yard. Tool, with Tamalita and Angel, were behind him. Bringing up the rear was ChaCha, Juanito, and Carolina.

Cruising north up Green Bay Road, Macho nodded his head to Da Brat's *"FUNKDAFIED"* as it pounded from the six 12-inch JL Audio W7s in the plush sleeper. Romeo watched as Macho shifted the transmission, taking notes on how smoothly he did it. He noticed that Macho hadn't once used the clutch to shift a gear, and he paid close attention to how Macho only used the splitter switch, right where his thumb was, to split only the four gears in the high range.

Macho could tell Romeo was watching, so he made sure to fully display what he had did. The best teacher one could have was themselves. The hunger to learn fueled ambition, and ambition is what gave you the drive.

In Zion, ten minutes later, Macho passed his woman's subdivision, their property, then came to 9th Street. Flipping the switch on the dashboard, he turned the jake brake on. Romeo got goosebumps from how loud and angry Macho's truck sounded, and every time he broke it down a gear, the jake got louder.

Making a wide left turn after a few southbound-traveling vehicles passed, Macho coasted down the hill, jake brake on, keeping him from going too fast. The others turned behind him and rode their jakes down the hill as well.

The wide entrance to the five-acre gravel lot of Freddie Fred's Diesel Power, LLC, came up on the left. Through the tall chain-linked fence, Romeo could see a huge 125,000-square-foot garage with ten bays, most of them opened up; a few cab semi-trucks with dump trailers were parked next to each other off to one side.

Up at the office, a building that was not attached, a big Freightliner tow truck, two small service trucks, and the owner's convertible 1970 Plymouth Hemi Cuda—its gleaming Lemon Twist yellow paint shining like the golden sun up in the sky, with ultra-bright white leather interior—were parked. A brand new Porsche 911 Carrera Cabriolet, sporting Racing Yellow. All of them were luxury and foreign-made. Just like the Valdez family-owned businesses, all other companies owned and run by close friends and associates treated their employees right. Without their workers, life would be very hard.

Macho swung his rig left and got turned around, backing the trailer up and parking ten feet away from it. In his mirror, Macho could see the restored old school in the garage, waiting to be loaded onto his trailer, as well as five others. Tool got turned around and backed to the second bay, then ChaCha at the third, and Juanito in front of the fourth.

Macho had Romeo get the iPad and put the log into "On Duty / Not Driving; Loading" duty status, stopping the drive time. As they opened their doors to get out, the glossy royal blue Pride & Class Peterbilt 389 owned by Javi, pulling a step decker, turned into the lot, with the jake brake roaring out of big 10-inch stacks. The 2015 Pete was the green-eyed Dominican's baby; all the Valdez boys decked their main rigs out, and Javi had did his right.

Macho chuckled as the Pride & Class beefed-up ISX Cummins engine revved up as Javi showed out. Thick plumes of black diesel smoke shot up out the pipes as 1,100 horses sounded off.

Train horns then blasted as the flashy rig swung around to back up to the fifth bay. The door behind Macho opened up. He turned around and saw the 60-year-old man of the hour coming out of his office.

"Freddie Fred! What's good, Unc!" Macho said, geeked to see the big, burly, equally tall man. Fred was dark brown, with salt n' pepper hair cut into a neat bald fade. His face, clean-shaven, void of wrinkles. He looked young for his age. The man had been like a brother to Macho's grandfather. Back when they were young, and moving cocaine by the truckload all over the country, Fred had been the one keeping trafficking big rigs rolling—designing hidden gun racks to put in them, developing secret armoring—and when he wasn't in the garage, he was hauling loads of coke himself.

When Fred and his wife had brought their daughter into the world, Juanito and Diego had Fred leave the dirty work to them. They loved Fred like a brother and didn't want inevitable drama coming to him, his wife, nor their new baby.

Fred delved into diesel technology and eventually built his own diesel repair business and established a reputation for restoring old trucks, bringing them into the new age.

"Hey there, nephew! Thanks for comin'," Fred said, embracing Macho as the others walked up. "You been alright, youngster?"

"You know me, Unc," Macho told him.

"That is exactly why I asked." Fred chuckled to himself.

Macho shook his head. He introduced Fred to Romeo and told him he was the newest to join the crew.

"Good to meet you, young man." Fred shook Romeo's hand.

"Likewise, sir. This is a nice place you got here," Romeo said.

"Thank you. A lot of hard work will get things like this for you. Remember that, and you'll go far."

Tool, ChaCha, the ol' heads all came up and either dapped or hugged the ol' head. Javi, his wife, and their kids got out of his Pride & Class and came over as well.

The office door opened again. Behind the two three-month-old Doberman Pinscher pups was Fred's beautiful daughter.

She was stunning, to say the least. Her skin was brown sugar-toned like that of Michelle's. Her eyes were the shapes of walnuts. Her little nose had a small diamond stud in it, and her dark brown hair was braided in neat boxed single braids, pulled back into a ponytail. Standing 5'6", she was blessed with a near-perfect coke bottle figure. The 20-year-old and her father were very close, and in recent times, they'd suffered a devastating loss. Fred's wife—Beautiful's mother—had been killed in a violent car crash involving a police car chase. Cops had been chasing a murder suspect, and, in a case of wrong place, wrong time, the Summers family queen was hit hard by the speeding getaway car while she cruised on her way home to her husband and daughter.

"Beautifuuuul! I just want you to know, that you're my baby siiiis!" sang Macho, remixing Snoop Dogg and Pharrell's hit song.

Gob smacked by Beautiful, Romeo was stuck. He'd never seen such perfection before.

She is... beautiful! he thought to himself, as Beautiful walked towards Macho with a poker face.

"Lil Sis, what up, yo!" Macho said, with wide-open arms.

WHAM!

"OOMF!"

The normally quiet, yet comical Beautiful shot a hard jab into Macho's sternum, knocking the wind out of him.

Tool, Javi, Michelle, Tamalita, Javi Jr., Amara, and everyone else busted out laughing as Macho doubled over at the hip, trying to refill his lungs with air.

"That's for not answering my texts or my calls, Antonio!" she told him. "Kim and Lacey have some for you too, asshole."

"Mm… my bad… s-sis," Macho stammered, still feeling her fist.

"Uh huh. Anyways!" she sassed, while everyone else continued snickering. "I was trying to call your big ass because," Beautiful paused, digging in her pocket to pull out her leather Prada wallet, "I GOT MY CLASS A LICENSE!" she then shouted excitedly.

Beautiful pulled out her fresh, hot-off-the-press Class A Commercial Driver's License with all the endorsements.

Tool cheered for her, scooping her up and swinging her around.

"THAT'S WHAT I'M TALKING 'BOUT, LIL SIS!" he shouted, hugging her now. "CONGRATULATIONS!"

Beautiful's accomplishment was celebrated by all of them. Macho, once he finally got air in his lungs, gave his baby play-sis a congratulatory hug.

"I'm proud of you, lil lady," he said. "What's next for you?"

Fred's pups started getting hyped up and jumped around Beautiful.

"Pete! Mack! Hush it up, now," Fred told them, as the other dogs started barking from the trucks.

"Daddy got me my own truck yesterday, bro," Beautiful said, pointing Macho's eyes over to where a row of trucks that Fred and his mechanics would be rebuilding.

"The Volvo?" asked Macho, seeing the big aquamarine-colored 780 with a big, high-rise sleeper berth.

"Yep! My big baby is so sexy!" gushed Beautiful.

"It better not be an automatic, yo," Macho said, eyebrows furrowing with accusing suspicion.

"Heelll no!" Fred answered for her. "My little girl wouldn't be caught dead in a punk-ass automatic! Those are for girls!"

Everyone busted out laughing at the man. Nobody in the Valdez family liked trucks with automatic transmissions, nor did any of their associates. Their motto was: *stick shift or kick shit!*

Beautiful gave her big play-brothers hugs—the ol' heads, ChaCha, Javi, and Michelle—giving Romeo a smile before hugging her father goodbye. She walked off and hopped into the sleek yellow Porsche and peeled off, like she had an extreme need for speed.

"That girl drives crazy," Fred said, as they all watched the Carrera blaze a trail up 9th Street towards Green Bay Road.

"She got it from you, ol' man," Juanito teased.

The family laughed.

"Hardy har har," Fred mocked. "Aye! Y'all come to laugh n' joke, or load up n' 'git? Time is money!"

"Truuueee!" shouted Macho. "Let's load up, family!"

An hour later, Macho, Tool, ChaCha, Juanito, and Javi all had their trailers loaded with rebuilt ol' school semis.

On Macho's trailer, a two-tone tan and green 1970 International Transtar was chained down. Blocks of wood were put at the wheels as added precaution; Tool had a 1981 Mack Superliner on *El Viejo's* trailer; ChaCha had a prehistoric dinosaur of a 1962 Kenworth W900 on her trailer; Juanito had a 1983 Chevy Bison, virtually the same as his GMC General—much like modern Chevrolet and GMC vehicles. On Javi's trailer, two 1980 Freightliner day cab cabovers that reminded Macho of the old black one in the movie *Terminator,* that the machine chased the kid on the dirt bike with, in a concrete channel.

Everyone got their destinations and Bill of Ladings for their leads. Bidding adieu to Fred, they all left. Macho was heading to Pontiac, Illinois—a short run, but would still net his company $6,500 for just a 2½–3 hour run.

G-Baby had booked him a backhaul as well. He'd have a load to pick up down in Peoria that had to go up to Racine, Wisconsin, adding $10,000 to the day's take.

G-BABY

"So no word from bro?" G-Baby asked, as she started downshifting gears with her truck's jake brake on, working the foot brake pedal to slow her rig on the curved off-ramp that'd lead her to the OshKosh Manufacturing plant, up in OshKosh, Wisconsin, close to 2 and a half hours north of the yard.

Sitting in the passenger's seat, Esmeralda, enjoying the ride, anxious to get back behind the wheel and secure herself a position in Numero Uno Transport.

They both heard Yessy's sigh come through the cab's speakers.

"No. I hope everything's okay with him, yo. He's been in a real funk over his wife," Yessy told her.

"Veronica is crazy, sis," Esmeralda chimed in. "He brought her and the kids to me and my man's house for a barbeque once; she's nuts."

"Well…." Yessy was clueless as to what to say.

G-Baby got onto a main road and could see the gargantuan plant she was going to.

"I left him emails and texts," Yessy said. "Fingers crossed, y'all."

"Yup. How's the class goin' anyways?" asked G-Baby, coming up to the entrance, where she saw the rear of Xavier's truck as he waited to gain entrance.

Yessy told G-Baby how boring the reintegration class was. Remembering it, from having to have had to attend themselves, G-Baby and Esmeralda laughed.

They finished their call as Xavier pulled in. G-Baby pulled up to the security booth and handed her iPad over. The digital load manifest was checked out by the guard inside. Confirming her truck number and load info, he handed the iPad back and wished her a good day.

G-Baby thanked the man and rolled into the city-sized plant when the gates opened up. Already there: Tati, Maria, Lauren, Analise, and Anaka. Four other heavy haul trucks, bearing *Valdez Transport, LLC*, with the company's D.O.T. numbers and the MC numbers on their doors or sleepers. They were from the heavy haul division of Javi's company, which was run by Xavier.

Having to back into one of the buildings in a section designated for military vehicles, the *Numero Uno* ladies each took forty minutes or so to get loaded and pull back out.

Tati, Maria, Lauren, Analise, Anaka, and one of Xavier's guys named Thurgood got giant boxy-shaped M1070s. They were mammoth Army semi-trucks with four axles, big off-road wheels, built to pull massive lowboy trailers that would transport 135,000-pound M1 A1 Abrams battle tanks. Xavier and his other two guys got huge M1075 A1s that weighed more than 50,000 pounds each.

After they emerged, G-Baby was ready to get her own load. She backed her rig in with expert skill. The bulky off-road MK23 6X6 cargo carrier truck looked like a semi on steroids, with a flatbed mounted over the two rear axles. Despite it being shorter than the other military trucks the others picked up, G-Baby's load weighed an astounding 62,000 pounds—not even loaded.

Putting her brakes on, shifter in neutral, G-Baby reached out to the dashboard and hit a switch that was labeled "Air Dump Valve," causing the air in her tractor's rear suspension airbags to release, so when she started the lengthy process to break her RGN down, the LowBoy's deck would lower all the way to the ground before she pulled the gooseneck hitch apart from it.

Esmeralda put G-Baby's log onto "Not Driving / Loading," then G-Baby cut her engine off.

They were getting out with work gloves when another rig backed inside. G-Baby saw the dark blue 780 Volvo, pushing a tandem axle lowboy, built with a flip axle, back into the spot next to G-Baby.

On its sleeper, *PJ & D Transport* was decaled. Knowing how common it was to see a *PJ & D* rig—since the Valdez family's colossal 5,000-truck fleet company ran all 50 states—G-Baby thought nothing of it, until she caught a glimpse of the driver.

She instantly froze as the 780 stopped, brakes applied and engine cut off. Seeing red in mere seconds, G-Baby instantly had visions of running over and beating the living shit out of the driver.

"Gabi, what's wrong?" asked Esmeralda, noticing the angered look on the Gangsta Boo's face.

G-Baby was so heated that she couldn't even respond. All she could do was stare.

Esmeralda's brows furrowed. The sound of the driver getting out of the truck made her look towards the front of the rig. Seconds later, she saw what looked like a shorter replica of G-Baby round the front of the big Volvo, dressed in a pink shirt with *PJ & D Transport* on the front, tight blue jeans, and pink Timberlands. Her hair was braided in four big braids to the back, with three little braids in between them.

Esmeralda looked at G-Baby with shock, then the *PJ & D* driver, and back at G-Baby. "Gabi?" she said, looking for clarity.

Staring daggers into the pink'd out girl, G-Baby wore a tainting smirk. She came to within half a foot of G-Baby and stopped.

"What's up, sis," Mariela said. "Small world, runnin' into you here."

"She most definitely has," Michelle added, remembering many talks when she, Yessy, G-Baby, ChaCha, Evelyn, Gloria, and all the other ladies in the Valdez family inner circle had girl nights. Romeo was so geeked to know that soon, his sister was going to be crying tears of joy, jumping up and down with happiness.

"Naw, if we could just find the Gangsta Boo a man, then all would be well in the world," Javi said, picking his yawning daughter up.

Macho felt a rush of angered heat hit him out of nowhere at that. Michelle, knowing her cousin-in-law as well as her husband did, caught the way his eye twitched.

"Oh God...El Tiguere tiene sentimientos por ella… no es bueno," she thought to herself, hating the idea of Macho, Yessy, and G-Baby's bombproof friendship being blown to smithereens due to lust.

"So... when's Diamond due, cuz?" Macho asked, changing the topic.

"A month, approximately," Michelle told him. "Don't worry, you still have first pick."

"Maybe Gabi needs a pet, more than a man," he said.

"Para," Javi told his cousin.

Macho looked at Javi and saw suspicion in his emerald eyes. "Time to go, yo," Macho said. "Come on, Rome. You're drivin', and if you fuck my truck up, I'ma take the Escalade and paint it pink."

G-BABY

"Tranquil! You are a boss! Chill, ma!" snapped Yessy, her voice booming through G-Baby's Bluetooth headset, as she and Esmeralda chained the 6X6 down on her lowboy's deck, doing everything she could to ignore her sister, as Mariela guided a plant employee up onto her step deck in the M1070 she had been dispatched to pick up. "Think, Gabriela! Colonel Pane would be pissed that we made him look bad, after he stuck his neck out for us!"

G-Baby sighed as she finished tightening the chain that held the 6X6's rear driver's side corner. She knew Yessy was right, but she still wanted to beat Macho's ass one good time. "Did Antonio say anything else about the photo?" she asked Yessy, changing the topic.

"No. I'm telling you, though, sis… whoever this little dude is, it's like...Antonio dove into a fountain of youth and became a toddler again. I can't believe that he says it's not him."

G-Baby chuckled. "Lemme find out he had a baby with some bitch on the low."

"Yoooooo, on my motherfucking momma, I would kill him!" Yessy said. "I can't even handle knowing that he touched other bitches before me, Gabi! Him having a kid! With some other chick! On everything I love, yo, it would be on n' popping, B! Yahm sayin? Curtains for everybody, yo!"

"Whoa, whoa, whoa! Relax, sis!" G-Baby could feel her homegirl's fury through the phone. "You know Antonio wouldn't do you like that. He ain't got eyes for no woman but you, jow. Yo' ass wildin' even thinkin' that."

For a minute, as Esmeralda continued prepping the 6X6 to be transported—11 feet tall, 8 feet wide, and 24 feet long—it filled the 25-foot-long well in the center of the lowboy, where cargo sat up perfectly. G-Baby heard no reply from Yessy.

"You there, sis?" G-Baby asked, wondering if she'd lost service.

"This is what's gonna happen," Yessy finally said. "You and Mariela are teaming those loads together to the Great Lakes base. You and Mariela are going to kiss and make up, because she is going to be coming to Numero Uno as a driver."

"WHAT?" shouted G-Baby, her voice grabbing the attention of nearly everyone in the building. "Gabi. Sis. Yo, you know I love you with all my heart, but life is too short for the bullshit. Like, come on, ma! Y'all beef about dumb gang shit was damn near 15 years ago! Let it go! And you… you need more love in your life. You won't let no man get you right, so why not let your baby sister into your life, yo!"

"Yessy!"

"No! He dicho!" Yessy stated.

G-Baby busted out laughing. "Okay, Dr. Ana Maria Polo," she clowned, referring to Yessy as the no-nonsense judge on the wild-ass Spanish court TV show *"Caso Cerrado."*

"Jódete, cabrona." Yessy chuckled. "For real though, yo. Dead that shit, Gabi. For me and Antonio."

She sighed. "Okay. For y'all. Talk to you later, punk ass."

Yessy laughed. "Love you, sis."

"I love you, too."

"Everything cool?" Esmeralda asked, taking her gloves off.

"Yeah. I have to go do something real quick," G-Baby said, looking at her sister.

Mariela was just finishing putting yellow *Oversize Load* banners on the back of her trailer. Esmeralda watched G-Baby walk over to her sister. For a few seconds, the two looked at each other. Cringing as she anticipated a bloody brawl, Esmeralda breathed a sigh of relief when she saw G-Baby open her arms and wrap them around her sister.

"Now that's what's up," the Syrian chick said, smiling now at the sight before her. "All she needs is a man, then her world is all good."

MACHO

He grinned at the pictures of the two customized foreigns sent to his email. The company he selected to do them up was the most top-notch in Miami. He couldn't wait to see the look on his woman's—and on G-Baby's—faces when he gifted them to them. Together, the two vehicles had cost him close to $700,000, but for the two ride-or-die chicks, money was no issue. Macho loved doing for them.

Rick Ross's "SORRY," featuring Chris Brown, bumped as Romeo traveled south on I-55 from Pontiac. He was geeked to be driving Macho's truck. With it having an 18-speed transmission, Romeo thought it was going to be hard to drive—until Macho walked him through it. At first, Romeo thought the shifter was to move eighteen times, but as Macho explained, Romeo learned that the shifter only moved nine times.

"On the low side of the transmission, there's five gears, and on the high side, there's four. Each gear has a low and a high, which essentially doubles each gear by the red splitter switch on..." he remembered Macho telling him at the soybean farm.

Using his memory from watching Macho shift gears, Romeo actually did pretty good. Minimal grinding of gears, and he knew how to shift without the clutch, only using it while stopped or downshifting gears to slow down or stop.

Reaching Chenoa, Macho had Romeo get off of 55 and take Route 24 west, all the way to Peoria Heights, then had him shoot down to East Peoria.

Still trailing behind: Javi and his family. They all made their way to the Caterpillar plant and picked up new D6T bulldozers. After loading up, Macho got back behind the wheel, not feeling that Romeo was ready to pull a load yet, before getting his shifting down pat.

Shooting back north to the Heights, then back west on 24 to 55, they got back on 55 and headed northbound. Just after five in the evening, Yessy called. Macho answered, finding himself way past excited to hear from her.

"Dímelo, maintaaaa! ¿¡Qué pasóooooo!?"

Her laughter filled the cab with the sound that Macho loved more than the roar of a powerful Caterpillar engine.

"Hey! You sound happy to hear from me," she said.

"¡Claro que sí, amor! ¡Ya tú sabes!" he hollered.

"Well, damn! I must be special!"

"You ain't know?"

"Yeah, I did. I just wanted to hear you say it, punk."

Macho and Romeo laughed.

"How'd he do today?" Yessy asked.

"He did pretty damn good, love. I think he's ready to go take his permit test."

Romeo started grinning.

"Cool. Soooo… guess what?" Yessy said.

"Dime," replied Macho.

"I got Gabi and Mari to kill that beef and make up."

"¡No joda!" Macho gasped in shock. "¿¡En serio!?"

"Muy serio, papi. And um, I kind of stole Mari from PJ & D."

"Oooooo... you better take yo weight, Yessy. ChaCha gon' kick your ass, bae."

"No she's not, Antonio. I talked to her before I hollered at Mari. Mena supports my decision to get Gabi and her sister together."

"I do too. It'll be good for G-Baby to have sis rolling with her. Guess I gotta get two more trucks instead of one."

"Hey! Don't you mean three?" Romeo asked.

"Bro, you get a truck when you get your license. Until then, shush," Yessy told him.

"I'll beat cha ass, yo," he mumbled.

"Fuck you say?" she recanted.

Macho laughed so hard that he almost drifted into the lane next to him. Thankfully, there wasn't a vehicle in it.

"I thought that's what you said, Big Head."

"Where you at, bae? Home?"

"Um... I was, but I had to step out for a second."

Macho's eyebrow rose up. "Step out?"

"Yes. Just needed to handle something really fast, papi. I'll see you two at the yard, okay?"

"Yeah yup." Macho grew frustrated with her.

"Don't get frustrated, Antonio."

"I'm not," he capped.

"Love you too, Yessy."

The call ended with Macho's mind racing.

"Your sister be on some extra shit sometimes, Rome."

Romeo busted out laughing at Macho. "That's your woman, bro."

Chapter 11

Fernando finished rolling his blunt of Kush and put some fire to it, to roast it dry. Next to him, his baby momma was rolling up another one to flame up after the first one. Music blared from the expensive home audio system in the living room of their loft apartment in Grayslake.

"You still haven't heard word yet, bae?" his woman asked him.

"No, Natalie, your brother still hasn't been found. He's probably running. His ass failed to murk dude, and Vito got people lookin' for him."

Natalie sighed. She and her brother had been recruited into an Ecuadorian crime syndicate, comprised mostly of drug trafficking and dealing. Her baby daddy had brought them in himself as help for when his big homie gave him missions. Recently, Natalie's brother Raul was sent to pop a very rich cocaine trafficking truck driver. He left to handle the business the previous night and hadn't been seen since. It was learned that his target was still alive, which was very bad.

"Spark that shit up, bae," she told her baby daddy. "I'ma go check on Cassie."

She got up and made her way to the stairs that led up to their loft bedroom. Climbing the stairs, Natalie reached the top, then screamed when she saw two women in all black—one holding her 1-year-old daughter, the other holding a shotgun.

"Cassie!" Natalie panicked, then screamed for her baby daddy.

The taller woman shook her head at Natalie, as she held the little girl in her arms.

"Fernando can't help you, ma," she said. "Ven aquí."

Natalie obeyed, going towards the woman, very aware of the shorter woman pointing the gauge at her.

"Mira," the girl with her child told her, nodding her head over the railing at the edge of the loft floor.

Natalie went and looked over. She gasped when she saw her baby daddy being held in a headlock by a huge man with dreadlocks.

Fernando struggled to get free as the giant's arms restricted the amount of air he could breathe. "No! Please! What do y'all want?" Natalie begged to know.

The woman with the baby looked at her, while Cassie cooed—way too young to understand what was going on.

"Your brother tried to kill my man and me while we were celebrating. We know you work for Vito Tavarez. Where does he live?"

"I don't know!" Natalie cried, looking at her baby.

The woman stepped close to the railing and held the baby up over it.

"Nooooo! My baby!" Natalie cried, lurching forward to grab her child.

The woman with the shotgun ran up on her and hit her in her temple with the butt of the Mossberg. Natalie flew to the floor, bleeding from the deep gash made by the gauge. "Get up, Natalie," the chick with her baby demanded.

Staggering to her feet, Natalie put her hand on the side of her head—blood leaked from the wound profusely.

The woman asked Natalie again for the whereabouts of the big dog.

"I swear! I don't know!" she said again.

Shaking her head, the woman shouted, "¡Pártele el cuello!"

"Nooooooo!"

Natalie ran to the banister and looked over, just as the giant deadhead snapped Fernando's neck like a twig. She cried for her baby daddy as his body dropped to the floor, leg twitching.

"Nandoooo!" Natalie screamed, devastated.

"Last chance, Natalie," the woman said.

"My baby daddy has his number! In his phone!" Natalie said.

The woman told the deadhead to look for Fernando's phone. He saw it on the table and grabbed it, then searching the contacts, he found Vito's number. He looked up and gave a thumbs-up.

"Okay, then." The woman looked at Natalie. "We're all done here, ma."

"Please! Give me my baby!" Natalie begged.

"Your daughter deserves a mother that doesn't become a sucker like you, yo," the woman told her.

BOOM!

The gauge blasted a deer shot, exploding Natalie's head. The loud noise made the baby scream out in fear as the headless corpse fell to the floor.

"Shhhhh. It's okay, mamas," the woman said, rocking the little girl lovingly. "You're gonna be okay, now that a good family is gonna take care of you."

Then the woman carried the whimpering baby to the stairs and descended them with the chick and the shotgun right behind her.

"Let's bounce, bro," she said to the deadhead. "We need to take little Cassie here to her new family, then get back to the yard."

"Me hope 'de little girl won't be scared 'a 'dat creepy ol' truck," the girl with the shotgun said.

The deadhead chuckled as he patted Cassie's hand, making her smile at him.

"Naw. Lil Mama got G in her heart, yo. *Homiez.*"

The two women then left out of the apartment. The dread pulled a small shoebox from out of the bookbag he'd brought. Setting it on top of Fernando's dead body, he opened the top and pressed the little red button on it, then ran out of the spot as the incendiary device did its job—setting a blaze so intense that as he reached the old Peterbilt, idling down a side street through a wooded area behind the complex, the whole loft had become a raging inferno.

G-BABY

After delivering the 6X6 to her old stomping grounds and seeing many of the soldiers she, Yessy, Esmeralda, and the other Numero Uno drivers had been in with, G-Baby headed back to the yard, with a meetup planned for her and her sister the next day.

Arriving back at the yard, she saw Macho and Romeo had just pulled in and had parked at the diesel fuel pumps the yard had.

G-Baby pulled her Kenworth to a pump as well, parked, put her log *"Off Duty,"* then she and Esmeralda got out.

His heart rate sped up when he saw her climb out of her truck with Esmeralda. He couldn't help but smile.

Maliante and Dreams ran over to the ladies, tails and butts wagging excitedly. G-Baby kissed their noses, then looked at Macho, seeing him staring at her.

***

Why why whyyyyy? Be ugly, man! she thought to herself as he made his way over toward her and Esmeralda.

"What's up, ladies? How'd it go?" Macho asked.

"All good," Esmeralda replied, patting Maliante's head. "I can't wait 'til I'm officially on with y'all."

"You already are, Esmeralda—the minute my lady gave you a call."

Nodding appreciatively, Esmeralda shook Macho's hand as he welcomed her to Numero Uno.

The sound of El Viejo's jake brake roaring grabbed everyone's attention toward where Wadsworth Road ran past the entrance to the yard. They saw the ol' school 359 Extended Hood turning into the yard seconds later.

MACHO

El Viejo entered the lot and pulled up to another diesel pump. The lights cut off, then the engine. Tool got out from behind the wheel, followed by Yessy. The dogs ran to her as Tamalita rounded the front of El Viejo with Angel on a leash.

Macho saw his woman was dressed in all black, looking like she was about to go hit a lick. He made his way over to her and gave her a kiss on the lips, then looked at her. "Why you look like you did something that I should've helped with?"

Yessy smiled shyly. "Because I did."

"Explain."

"Well, don't nobody wanna have some bomb-ass sex interrupted by a clown tryna shoot them, so I went to go find who sent him at us."

Macho shook his head.

"And... took a baby to a family that'll raise her in a house full of love, not violence."

"Oh wow."

"Whenever you ready, we can go get the bitch that really calls shots for the so-called Los Hombres Hechos," Yessy told him.

"Another day, love. Right now," he said, and paused, pulling her to him and kissing her again, making her moan and melt in his arms. "I just wanna take you home and make love to you... over."

He kissed her again. "And over."

He kissed her again. "And over again."

Yessy was on fire!

"Less talkin', more taking me home and doin' that—over and over and over again, papi," she said, pussy so wet that the crotch of her leggings looked like she pissed herself.

***

The next morning, Macho woke up to his woman, hunched over on her knees, swallowing his dick, deep-throating all ten inches like a pro. She had her ass tooted up high as she went hard on him.

The sight of her pleasing him while wearing a tight purple long-sleeved dress with an above-the-knee hem, black fishnet pantyhose with stars woven in them, and blue pointed toe ankle-strapped pumps on her feet, made his dick even harder in her mouth. Her hair was flat-ironed, parted up the middle, and pulled back into a sophisticated office-girl bun, and her lips were glossy red lipstick.

Yessy sucked her man off with true porn-star skill, spitting on it, licking from the tip down to the base, taking his balls into her mouth and sucking on them while jerking his cock with one hand. She made his toes curl so hard that he thought they'd break off.

"Ooohh shshshsheeeeeeiiiiit!" he cursed when he busted his nut.

Yessy jerked and sucked him dry. With a devious smile, she swallowed his cum, then licked her lips.

"Well, good morning, sleepyhead! Breakfast is ready. Get your booty up, brush your teeth, and come let me feed you while I suck your cock again before I go."

At that, Yessy got off the bed and switched her ass extra hard, encouraging him to hurry up and get a move on.

Over the next six days, Macho took Romeo on the road with him, teaching the young buck everything he could. Yessy got through her classes and was officially done with the Army.

On the seventh day, a trip to the DMV in Waukegan for Romeo to take the Illinois CDL knowledge test on the computer was combined with Yessy getting her Class A CDL with Air Brakes, Doubles/Triples, Tanker, Hazardous Material, and Passenger endorsements—all thanks to her Colonel submitting her commercial driving experience in the Army to the Illinois Secretary of State. Via the Even Exchange program, Yessy was able to get her CDL without taking a single test, and with her D.O.T. Medical card, she was now a certified civilian truck driver. Her brother was also now officially legal to practice driving.

For the following week, Yessy took her brother with her on trips, letting him drive unloaded and loaded. Macho and Javi teamed together, hauling supplies for schools, bringing in wood for new gym floors, industrial ventilation systems, and materials to make repairs to the actual buildings. During the week, the two donated a million dollars so that none of the kids in any grade had to pay for lunch for the entire year, nor for field trips or any other student events that would put strains on parents' budgets.

G-Baby and Esmeralda, along with ChaCha, Nena, Carolina, Juanito, Tool, Tamalita, and a few of the Numero Uno ladies, worked on the construction jobs Yessy and G-Baby had up in Racine, and two locations around northern Illinois that Y & G Realty's newest supervisor found and got for dirt cheap.

ROMEO

"Yo, come on, sis, where is we goin'?" Romeo asked, hating being kept in the dark.

"To see a house, dude! Stop whining!" Yessy told him, as she turned into her and G-Baby's subdivision.

Riding up the main street, Yessy passed by a few big houses with manicured lawns that still looked new, before reaching an area that was pale blue. Parked in the two-car-wide driveway that led to a 2½-car built-in garage was G-Baby, leaning up against the back of her SRT8 Jeep.

Playing in the yard with a ball were Javi Jr. and Amara. Dreams and Maliante were trying to join in, chasing the ball and getting faked out every time one of the kids threw the ball to each other.

"Yo, this a nice ass crib, Yessy. On the real, when I get my money all the way up, I'ma get me a joint like this."

Yessy smiled at his words as they got out of her Pininfarina BMW M7.

The dogs ran to her. The kids ran behind them to Yessy, excited to see her. G-Baby walked up to Romeo, hugged him, then gave him a set of keys.

"We're givin' this house away to this young dude that's been buildin' himself up the right way, and since you're his age, yo' sister and I feel like you could give us a good opinion if he'll like it."

"What am I? A real estate agent?" Romeo joked, just as a glossy blue Porsche Cayenne Turbo pulled up, turning into the driveway.

They all looked at the Porsche truck as the driver opened the door. A high heel with spikes at the toe got out, followed by a foot and leg encased in sheer black pantyhose.

Emerging from the Cayenne was the redhead Cuban-Armenian head of Y & G Realty, rocking a silk Versace top with a leather pencil skirt. Her fiery back-length mane was flat ironed straight and hung loosely down her shoulders. She wore just a little makeup and the gold and diamond Tiffany & Co. necklace that Xavier had gotten her right before she pulled a disappearing act.

Kenzie hurried over to the posse with her Ermenegildo Zegna satchel, looking flustered.

"Hey? You okay?" asked Yessy, giving the mother of Xavier's youngest child a hug.

"Yeah… had to make a bathroom stop," Kenzie told her, looking embarrassed.

Yessy sighed. She and the family knew about Kenzie's problem with the frequent trips to the ladies' room. The redhead was cursed with an incurable bowel disease called Crohn's. It affected her in ways that gave her limited time to get to a toilet—fast—when she had to go, or she was shit out of luck.

Despite many times failing to get to a bathroom before she missed her chance, Xavier had loved her to no end, which surprised Kenzie. Her oldest daughter's father had turned evil on her once he found out about the disease. He ridiculed her, disrespected her, and got physical with her to the point that Kenzie had contemplated suicide. If it wasn't for her firstborn, she doubted she'd be alive.

"It's okay, ma. You know you're good," Yessy said encouragingly to Kenzie. "You ready?"

Nodding, Kenzie took a deep breath and walked up to Romeo.

"After you, young man," she told him with a professional smile on her face.

The first floor was designed as an open concept. Veined marble floors, the walls painted deep blue to match the veins, the high ceiling and baseboards painted white to go with the marble.

The living room was very spacious and adjoined to the exclusive chef's-style kitchen, done up with more marble, Italian-made cabinetry, and name-brand stainless steel appliances. The kitchen had a dining area with a floor-to-ceiling glass retracting patio door that led out to the big backyard from a stone-built patio deck.

Up on the second floor, there were three guest bedrooms and a big master bedroom. Just at the top of the stairs was an opened-up lounge area that had a built-in projection system for movies to be played on the wall-sized screen across from it.

Last, they all went down to the basement. There was a big entertainment area built with a wet bar, a pool table, ping-pong table, another movie projector with theater-quality surround sound. There were three other multipurpose rooms that could be turned into exercise space, an office, or whatever else.

After following Romeo back up the stairs to the first floor, the ladies, the kids, and the dogs waited for his word.

"Yeah, sis, this crib is definitely up, yo," he told Yessy. "Dude who gon' get this will love it, 'yah mean? Who is he?"

"You," said Yessy, as she, G-Baby, and Kenzie started grinning.

Romeo's eyes went wide. "Wh-what? Yo, word!"

"Word, kid," Yessy nodded. "That little apartment ain't cutting it, and I want you out here with us."

"Wow." Romeo went to his sister and threw his arms around her, hugging her ecstatically. "Thank you, sis! On the real, yo! I love it!"

"It's all good, lil bro. You earned it."

"True," G-Baby agreed. "You have a 4,200-square-foot home at just 22 years old. You doin' it, lil dude."

"Wish I had this when I was 22," Kenzie chuckled. "But four years ago, I was barely makin' it for my daughter and me, with our little one-bedroom apartment over in Horizon Village." Kenzie reached out and touched his shoulder. "You are blessed, Romeo. Thank the man above every day you wake up for what you have—and even what you don't have."

Romeo nodded his head in understanding. He could literally feel the passion in her words as she spoke.

G-Baby stepped close to Yessy and whispered, "That girl is gonna be Xavier's wife. Care to place a wager on that?"

Yessy shook her head. "Absolutely not," she replied, feeling the same way. "Romeo, I think there's something in the garage for you, yo."

In a flash, Romeo was gone. He truck-star'd it to the door that led to the garage and opened it. The second he saw what was there, he frowned.

"The fuck?" he said to himself, seeing absolutely nothing but a bare garage.

Yessy, carrying Amara, G-Baby holding Javi Jr.'s hand, Kenzie, and the dogs showed up seconds later.

"Why you playin', sis?" Romeo asked Yessy, turning to see that she and the others were smiling at him. "Where the Bentley and the Rolls at, man?"

"At the dealership, baby boy," G-Baby told him.

"Romeo, I gave you a $100,000 Cadillac truck, sittin' on rims worth damn near $30,000, and now a $335,000 house," Yessy listed. "The ball is in your court now, yo. You gotta be the one to get that cheese and cop that Bentley and that Rolls Royce."

"Buuut... there is one more thing we have for you," G-Baby added, just as they all heard the sound of a truck engine outside of the garage.

Yessy hit the garage door opener button on the wall. With puzzled brows, Romeo waited as the door rolled up.

Seconds later, he saw a shiny money-green rig in the middle of the street, looking like it just rolled out of the factory.

Macho got out from behind the wheel, rocking a diamond chain, a white T-shirt, tan Dickies, and all-white Retro Air Jordan 4s, with his hair free of braids, combed and pulled back into a bushy ponytail.

Yessy was instantly turned on by the sight of him hopping out of the rig.

So was G-Baby.

Javi came around the front of the rig as Macho reached the sidewalk, rocking a tan Dickies suit, his hair in a ponytail as well, with two diamond chains and white Air Jordan 1s on his feet.

"DAADDIIIE!" Amara shouted excitedly.

Yessy set her down and let her and Javi Jr. run to their pop. Javi scooped his babies up and smothered them with kisses.

Macho walked up to Romeo with a grin on his face. "All you, young buck," he told him.

"Th-that's... mine?"

"Yessuh! 2004 Freightliner Coronado 132, with the bubble-eye Benz headlights. Rebuilt Series 60 Detroit engine, 500 horses, 530 in torque, condo-style sleeper with double bunk beds, leather and wood interior, air-ride seats, air-ride suspension. It's a badass truck, lil cutty."

"And fast!" Javi said, walking up holding his children's hands.

"Got from Jersey to Pittsburgh to here in eleven hours."

"That's not fast, Javi, it's dumb!" Yessy countered, with twisted lips, looking from Javi to Macho, knowing why they'd gone to New Jersey, then to the Steel City before bringing Romeo's new ride back to the Ill State.

Macho sheepishly smiled as Dreams stood next to him, wagging her tail.

"It got to PDub safe and sound, baby," Macho reasoned, keeping Romeo in the dark about the truckload of cocaine he'd brought his childhood best friend/Steel City Mafia brother, once he and Javi had returned from taking big wooden crates full of cash to the Jersey docks, destined for his grandparents in the Dominican Republic.

"This time," Yessy said, then let it go. "But anyways," she continued, looking at her brother, "take your truck to the yard; everyone is waitin' for us. Antonio has something for all Numero Uno Transport drivers."

Romeo looked at Macho.

Macho nodded his head and winked at him. "See you in a minute, young buck."

Chapter 12

Romeo shifted the 13-speed transmission smoothly as he tested his new Coronado out. Though the actual truck was thirteen years old, the engine, transmission, clutch, suspension, and interior were all brand-new, manufactured a year before the Department of Transportation had mandated that engines made after the year 2000 be built with ELD (Electronic Logging Device) plugs. Since Romeo's truck couldn't have an e-log hooked up, he would have to use traditional paper logbooks to record his trips.

He smiled his ass off as he cruised behind his sister, nodding his head to Nas's "ONE MIC Remix." He felt like he was riding on a cloud. For a tractor that weighed over 20,000 pounds, the Coronado rode like a Corvette with ten wheels.

Arriving at the yard, Romeo was the last to turn in. G-Baby, with the kids and dogs; Kenzie, with Javi; Yessy and Macho led the newest rig in to join the rest of the fleet. All drivers were present and waiting.

Inside, Esmeralda's new ride—a 2008 Kenworth W900L that also came from Tool's Glider kit builder spot in Jersey—shined hard from the wash, wax, and detail job she had just given it after her run down to Georgia's Fort Benning to deliver parts for the military base's vehicles. Romeo then saw a glossy black Chevy Avalanche sitting on big rims that matched the fixed-up ride. It was unfamiliar to him.

Pulling his Coronado up to where Esmeralda stood at the driver's side of her large car, Romeo parked, just as a light brown-skinned man got out of the Avalanche with two big puppies. Romeo had to do a double take when he saw the guy. The man looked so much like Macho that he thought somehow Macho had magically vanished from his sister's side and appeared in the Chevy truck.

The differences were that the guy was a little slimmer and just a few inches shorter. His hair was long and in fresh braids. He was tatted up from what Romeo could see and walked with swag as he made his way to meet an excited Yessy and G-Baby.

YESSINIA

"Enriquuee!" she shouted, running toward her military big bro.

G-Baby ran with her, as did Esmeralda. The three squealed in delight when the caramel-skinned man threw his arms around them. Romeo was slightly troubled when he saw his sister and G-Baby gravitating to another man like that. Glancing over at Macho and Javi, neither of them looked bothered. Kenzie looked a little puzzled, likely because Romeo figured she didn't know who the guy was either.

"Come on, youngster." Macho patted Romeo's shoulder, ushering him on with Javi, the kids, and himself to meet the guy.

"Enrique, this is my baby brother Romeo," Yessy introduced. "And Romeo, this is Enrique, A.K.A.. DBoy."

"DBoy?" Rome questioned, with a glance at Macho. "Like, as in Dope Boy?"

DBoy chuckled.

Yessy nodded her head for him to explain his nickname. "Naw, lil bruh. I go by DBoy because I was Delta Force in the Army. The Green Berets and other units called us all DBoys. It just stuck with me."

"Delta Force… I heard of them before," Romeo said, trying to remember when.

"They're the only unit in the United States military that can wear plain clothes and grow their hair out to execute covert operations," G-Baby told him.

"And Delta Force is also the unit that caught and killed Pablo Escobar," added Esmeralda. "This guy right here… not good to be on his bad side."

"Which is great for us," Yessy concluded, hugging DBoy again.

Romeo studied the guy for a minute. He put him at about 5'9", maybe 180 pounds or so. He looked Arabic, which was funny to Romeo since DBoy had braids.

"Are you Middle Eastern?" Romeo asked him.

"My mother was born in Beirut, Lebanon, but my father was Brazilian from Rio."

"How old are you?" Romeo then asked.

"Thirty-two," DBoy told him. "Got two kids: a six-year-old son named after me and my nine-year-old daughter named Alejandra. Their mother, Veronica, is from Venezuela but raised in Harlem like I was."

Romeo could hear the accent in DBoy's words now that he was really listening. He was happy to meet another New Yorker—especially one that had the approval of his sister and Macho—and as the others came over, greeting DBoy emphatically, he knew that the man was somebody to everyone there.

Yessy told her brother about how DBoy had taken her and G-Baby under his wing when they'd gone down to Fort Leonard Wood in Missouri. He was soon to be going to Fort Bragg to join the Special Forces unit, which ultimately led to him joining Delta Force, the most elite land unit the military had. Until then, though he'd been a truck driver in the Army, he later became a trainer. He trained so many soldiers how to drive commercial trucks and buses in the six years he'd been at Fort Leonard Wood that he'd lost count. He even trained soldiers to recognize possible IEDs in the road by seeing where holes might have been dug up to hide roadside explosives and to be defensive drivers.

Yessy and G-Baby were beasts behind the wheel of any vehicle with wheels or caterpillar tracks, thanks to DBoy—and many of their fighting skills came from him as well.

"Have I gained 'ya approval?" DBoy asked Romeo.

Romeo nodded his head. "You cool."

"Well, alrighty then! Everybody! I got something for y'all, yo!" Macho said to the Numero Uno crew.

Romeo saw him run to where his Mulliner-spec'd Bentley Mulsanne was parked and retrieve the briefcase that he'd been given by Michelle at the soybean farm a couple of weeks ago. Remembering what was inside, Romeo started smiling, unable to wait to see the look on everyone's faces.

The Numero Uno crew made a circle around Macho, his woman, and G-Baby. Yessy held the briefcase as he unlatched it. Pulling one of the little boxes out, he handed it to Chloe, telling them all not to open any of them until everyone had a box in their hand.

The main seventeen got one—Esmeralda, DBoy, along with Romeo, Yessy, G-Baby, and Macho.

Macho counted down from three, then the crew opened the boxes.

"Oh snap!" said DeeDee, with eyes as wide as dinner plates.

"Whoa!" Analise shrieked in shock.

"¡Diablos!" exclaimed Tatianna.

Victoria started laughing. "Nuts! Yo, this is dope, but funny as hell!"

Inside each box were completely custom-made gold championship rings, embedded with flawless baby diamonds. The tops of them had Numero Uno Transport's initials spelled in diamonds.

"Yeah, baby!" Brittany shouted, holding up a fist to show off her ring. "N.U.T., muthaffff…" She panicked when she saw the kids there next to their father. "Freakeerrr!" she finished.

Macho spoke. "Yo, as long as y'all have those on or close to you, no matter what, you are safe. They got special abilities," he said, which made them all chuckle.

Everyone raised their fists up and shouted, "N.U.T. forever!" Then they all busted out laughing.

Macho had Michelle create the rings after having to put down a young Afghani heroin dealer. The gold and diamonds he came up on were his reward for the job, given by the Arab dope boy's own uncle. Remembering the scene in one of his favorite movies, *State Property*—starring Beanie Sigel—where "Beans" gifted his ABM crew with custom rings, Macho wanted to do that for his people. Each ring was worth $50,000. He knew for a fact that by this time next year, everyone would still have their unique rings.

MACHO

The next day, Macho and Romeo met with DBoy at the yard. DBoy arrived in his Avalanche with his pups, parking next to Romeo's Escalade. DBoy was being taken to pick up his own heavy haul rig, bought by Macho.

"What type of dogs is them, DBoy?" asked Romeo, thinking they were pit bulls but not sure due to how big they already were at just six months.

"Bully Kuttas," DBoy told him, dapping Macho up. "They're Pakistani Mastiffs. If you're thinkin' they're some pit bulls, it's because the breed has bull terrier in the lineage, like many other Mastiff types."

"They gon' get big as hell, right?" Macho asked, as the bigger of the two—brown with black tiger-stripe patterns all over him, ears clipped, and his body already muscular—sat next to DBoy's right leg.

The smaller one, fawn-colored, ears clipped, muscular as well, was the more energetic one. He was raring to run around, looking at DBoy for permission to go.

"They definitely are, yo. This big guy here is Bruce," he said of the calmer one. "And I call his little brother Torpedo."

"Torpedo?" Romeo questioned.

DBoy pulled a small plastic bag with Milk-Bone treats inside. He took one out, called Torpedo's attention. Torpedo's ears pricked up in alert, then DBoy held the treat up.

"Waaatch it! Waaatch it!" DBoy held it up, making Torpedo follow it with his eyes. DBoy then threw the treat as hard as he could. Torpedo took off running as if indeed fired out of a destroyer. He met the treat nearly 50 feet away, jumped up, and caught it.

"Well okay, then," Romeo said, understanding now.

***

"Yo, what up?" Macho answered when Narco called.

In his Mulsanne, Macho cruised toward Javi's yard to meet up with his cousins. The call came in as he passed 9th Street, coming up on where a massive landfill sat across from a gigantic scrapyard.

"The time is upon us, bro," Narco said. "Amarillo. Tomorrow. Leave at night to avoid state troopers and the weight stations."

Reaching the light at Russell Road, Macho got into the left-turn lane and paused for it to turn green.

"You're tellin' a truck god how to move on the highway? Really?"

"I'm just sayin', Macho: I need this to make it to me. It's important. You know my bitch-ass dad cut me off. My money lookin' real funny, bro."

"Don't worry, my boy." Macho made his turn once the light turned green. "It's me—The Macho Man!"

Narco laughed. "I thought yo' ass was gon' say 'EL Tigure!' like you always do."

"That's for my lady. Speakin' of ladies," Macho said as a thought popped into his head. "How come I haven't heard from Nadia? Ain't she out yet?"

"Yeah, she out now. She been outta town for the last two weeks, though."

"Out of town?"

"Down below the border, tryna talk to my dad."

"Uh... is she alive?" Macho asked, as the light at the Russell and Kilbourne Road intersection came into view.

"Yeah, but her hopes of getting the ya-dig bank in order are dead."

Macho shook his head. "Well, that sucks."

"It is what it is, bro. When you get back from down there, ride up on me. You know it be poppin' out here this time of year, especially when Nadia brings her grill out."

"Mmmmmm.... Nadia food. Bet that, yo. Homiez, I'll be up."

"Yup. Love, too, 'foo," Narco said.

Macho busted out laughing as he made a right onto Kilbourne.

"Shut cho' ass up, man," Narco chuckled, knowing Macho was clowning how folks from Milwaukee ended talks.

"Right away, dog! Love, too, 'foo!" Macho mocked, then he ended the call.

G-BABY

At the garage, G-Baby awaited her sister to arrive. Her four-year employment as a driver for PJ & D was done, her two weeks' notice accepted, and her clean red Peterbilt 386 and step-deck trailer waiting for her to put on the road.

Romeo's Escalade pulled in and parked amongst the other drivers' vehicles. He got out wearing a Numero Uno shirt, jean shorts, Tims, and his hair in fresh braids to the back.

"What up, Joe?" G-Baby hugged him and laughed when he muffled her hair. "Stop, you ass!"

He laughed as she swatted at him. "You look like you waitin' for something."

"My sister."

"Eeeeee, yo, I heard she look just like you!"

G-Baby turned her head and glared at him. "No."

"No she doesn't look like you, or...?"

"No as in leave my sister alone, or I'ma molly whop yo' ass, dude."

"Well, damn! Violent-ass Puerto Rican!"

G-Baby heard a vehicle coming down the path road just then. She looked and saw her sister's clean Audi A8 rolling in.

"That's her?" Romeo asked, looking real hard to see the mini G-Baby.

"Romeo... I am not playing with you."

"I ain't on shit, Gabi. Chill, yo."

The Audi pulled up and parked next to Romeo's Cadillac truck. The driver's door opened up, and Mariela got out, looking like she was heading to the club.

ROMEO

Holy shit! Goddamn! Goddamn! G-baby's sister bad as fuck, yo! he thought as he drank the miniature G-Baby in.

Her long dark brown hair flowed freely down her back. The sleeveless Balenciaga top she had on let her tattooed arms show and had very open cleavage. She had on a leather Balenciaga miniskirt and Balenciaga heels that looked like open-toe socks with heels.

Romeo started salivating. Her voluptuous figure was perfect in his eyes. She had G-Baby's exotic, Asian-like eyes, big breasts, a slim waist, wide hips, thick thighs, and her legs glistened from a fresh wax and oiling.

WHAM!

"Ow!" Romeo rubbed the back of his head, looking at G-Baby. "The hell you smack me for, yo?"

"That's nothin' compared to what I'ma do if you try to put the woo on my sister, Romeo!"

"Sis!" Mariela shouted, putting a little pep in her step to get to her big sister. "Look at you, coming here all cute n' shit," G-Baby said, giving Mariela a hug.

Romeo was transfixed on Mariela. As the two hugged, Mariela, facing away from him, made it impossible for him not to look down at her big, juicy 44-inch ass.

Maaan, she got ASS ASS, yo! On God! he thought to himself, finding it impossible to look away. He bit his lip hard to will his dick to keep from getting hard.

Mariela let go of her sister, and having not noticed him before, looked at Romeo. Her eyes went big for a second when she locked with his.

"H-Hi," he stammered to say.

"Hey," she replied back timidly.

G-Baby stepped in between them, looking up at Romeo. "I think Anaka is waiting for you, Romeo!"

He shook his head. "Come on, yo. Don't even do that to me, Gabi. Me and Anaka are just friends."

"That had sex! And kissed!" G-Baby hated, glaring at him again. "Yeah, nigga! Everybody knows about you two, so stop playin'!"

Mariela giggled at the salty look on Romeo's face.

"Stop bein' mean to him, Gabi," she said, batting her eyes at Romeo.

"¡Que se joda si ese tipo es un mujeriego!" G-Baby said, still glaring at him.

"See y'all later, yo," Romeo said, not wanting any smoke with G-Baby.

"Byye," Mariela said, smiling at him.

WHAM!

"Ow! What the fuck, Gabi?" Mariela complained, rubbing the back of her head.

"Don't start bein' a thot, Maria! That's Yessy's little brother! Yessy's like my sis, so he's supposed to be like yo' brother!"

Romeo chuckled to himself, hearing G-Baby going in on her sister.

She diggin' the kid fa sho, yo. The look in her eyes say soon, I'ma be between them thighs, he thought as he got to his Coronado. His phone rang when he reached for the door handle. He pulled it out of his pocket and saw it was her. Geeked, he answered with a cheesy-ass smile. "Talk to me, Foxy Cleopatra," he joked.

Anaka laughed. "You're funny. Hurry up and come hit this pussy, baby. It's ready for you."

"Oh, I am on *thee* way, gorgeous. Have that thang wet for me, aight?" he said, climbing up into the cab.

"Baby, this good-good been wet for you since I woke up this morning."

Romeo ended the call with a huge smile on his face. He looked over at where the two sisters were. He saw Mariela climbing up the cab step to her truck. So much ass behind her that Romeo's dick started pulsating like it had its own heartbeat.

"Swear to God I'm at lil mama, yo. I gots to get it, B!" he said to himself, already thinking about how he could get at her without big sis cockblocking.

Chapter 13

MACHO

At the yard, just after nine o'clock that night, Yessy's eyes filled with tears. She was furious, angry enough to start wildin' out on him.

Still there, even after her sister left, was G-Baby, who was grinding her teeth in anger. She had half a mind to go run to get rope and duct tape to tie him to a chair so he couldn't leave. Also there was Tamalita. The Belizean belle was now a Belizean bull. She was infuriated with Tool. She didn't want him nor Macho to go.

"Yessy, stop crying," Macho told his lady, placing his hands on her shoulders.

"Then don't go!" Yessy snapped as tears fell down her face. "Please!"

"Yessy... relax. I will be okay."

"And I will not stop crying, mamao!"

Macho groaned with frustration. "¡Mi madre! ¡Qué vaina! ¡Me jodí ahora!"

"Because!" snapped G-Baby. "You be wildin', nigga! ¿Por qué no puedes usar la fucking cabeza, man?"

Macho shook his head. "I'm out, yo," he said, done with it.

Yessy's tears rolled down her face as she watched him step off.

"You're not even gonna say bye, or that you love me?" she asked.

He stopped walking. He turned his head halfway, and over his shoulder, he said, "See you when I get back... I love you, Yessinia."

With that said, Macho went and hopped up into *El Viejo.* They then watched a reluctant-to-go Tool go and climb up into the passenger's side of the Pete.

YESSINIA

"I love you, too, Antonio," Yessy said, as the floodgates opened up and tears poured down her face.

She and the others watched her man back *El Viejo* out of the bay, then roar off toward the exit. Half a minute after the Pete disappeared from their sight, they all could still hear his powerful Caterpillar engine, as Macho gunned it along Wedsworth Road toward the highway. G-Baby wrapped Yessy up in her arms in an effort to comfort her. Yessy wept, wanting to hop in her whip and go bring her man back by sheer force.

"Sis, I know you may not want to hear this, but... he is in *El Viejo,* and Tool is with him." Knowing firsthand everything done to the ol' school Peterbilt—and Tool being with Macho—did bring Yessy some comfort. She and G-Baby knew that *El Viejo* was the equivalent of an Abrams battle tank on ten wheels.

Yessy nodded her head. Maliante and Dreams both nudged her side, wanting to join in on the comforting of their human. They could sense her sadness.

She saw Tamalita a second later, standing by her lonesome. She had tears in her eyes. "Tama, come here, mamita," Yessy called to her.

Tamalita stepped into the duo's embrace, making it a trio. She burst into tears the second Yessy and G-Baby pulled her in. G-Baby willed her own eyes to stay tear-free, though it was killing her to know what Macho was about to do, and dragging his brother along with him.

Headlights appeared in the path road. They all looked up and saw Michelle's Ferrari LaFerrari rolling in. She came down and parked next to G-Baby's Jeep and hopped out, dressed in a white, gold, and blue silk Versace button-up long-sleeved shirt, with a black leather Versace pencil skirt, and blue Versace pointed-toe pumps on her feet. Her hair was spiral curled and hanging loose. Her gold jewelry was simple, but flicked hard.

She immediately saw how upset Yessy, Tamalita, and G-Baby were.

"Yo, what up wit y'all?" she asked, with concern etched into her face.

G-Baby told her what was up. Michelle, always having been very close to Macho, instantly grew infuriated.

"¡Coño! ¡Ese tipo 'ta loco! The fuck, yo?" she snapped, as she got her phone out of her Versace bag and made a call, putting it on speaker mode.

"Dímelo."

Yessy, G-Baby, and Tamalita all heard Tool's voice.

"Yo, your brother is really wildin'... again, Berto. That nigga's goin' down to frickin' Texas for his bitch-ass so-called friend to do you-know-what!"

They all heard Tool again. "I know. I'm with him, lil cuz."

"¡Ay, mi madre! ¡Qué carajo, Tool? What... the hell are y'all doing?"

"I'm askin' myself the same thing, yo."

Michelle ended the call, pissed all the way off. She looked at Yessy and Tamalita. "Okay, so, when they get back, I will be with y'all, so we can beat Antonio's ass. We are most definitely gonna have to jump him, 'cause that's a big-ass nigga, son, 'yahm sayin'?"

"I'ma do a lot more than beat that ass, yo!" said Yessy, as G-Baby wiped tears from her face. "That nigga ain't gettin' no toto for a week!"

"HA!" Michelle laughed. "Now *that* is bullshit, B. You can't go more than a few hours without letting him in ya front *and* ya back door, biatch."

G-Baby and Tamalita both laughed their asses off at Michelle, and the look on Yessy's face. Yessy smacked her lips. "Whatever. Ain't nobody ask ya short ass all that otha' shit."

Michelle laughed at her then.

MACHO

Young Jeezy's *Welcome Back* blasted as Macho put the pedal to the metal. The late hours of a Sunday night had the highways wide open. He blew through Lake County into Cook. From the Edens Expressway, he hit the Dan Ryan and put Chiraq behind him in less than half an hour. From the city, he switched onto the Stevenson and tore south on 55 to get to Missouri.

During the three-hour ride to the Poplar Street Bridge, Macho's thoughts were on the contents of the little red box that Michelle had made extra special. He was anxious to come across the right time to get on it. Out of everything he had done in his life—good and bad—this move would be the most memorable of them all.

He reached the Poplar Street Bridge and crossed over into Missouri, glancing at the Arch before coming upon the I-44 entrance junction to St. Louis. Jumping on 44, he kept on pushing. He passed Fort Leonard Wood, where his woman and G-Baby started their military truck driver careers. He smiled to himself, as memories of all the years that the two had been soldiers—photos with their unit, overseas, in danger zones, all smiles and big guns.

The times he thought they wouldn't return back to him. Times he had to go to military infirmaries when he learned they had been injured. Macho couldn't think of any other women as tough as the Bad Rican and the Gangsta Boo. It made him feel so incredibly guilty that he constantly dreamed of fucking G-Baby's brains out, over and over and over again.

Seeing signs for Joplin, Macho got into the granny lane to exit. He needed a break after turning a ten-hour run into eight, and the massive Petro 44 truck stop was his favorite stop spot in Missouri. He got off the interstate and made his way to the enormous truck stop. Before he parked, he fueled *El Viejo's* tanks up at the Phillips 66 diesel station, then found a spot to park the ol' school Pete. He and Tool got out and made their way inside, immediately seeing an extensively customized Peterbilt in the big shopping plaza. They checked out the glossy lime-green 379 Extended Hood and wondered if the famous custom truck builders, the Chrome Shop Mafia, had built it.

They went to use the restrooms, then made their way to the big Iron Skillet restaurant. After they placed their orders, Macho pulled his phone out and called his woman. Tool busted out laughing at him.

"I knew you's gon' call her, yo. Watch—she gon' get on ya bumper," he said, as he heard it ring for a third time.

"Nigga, she know better than that," Macho said.

Yessy answered. "Motherfucker! ¡Te lo juro por dios, cuando regreses te voy a caer encima, cabrón!"

Tool laughed so hard that his eyes filled with tears.

Macho sucked his teeth at him. "Shut up, nigga." Macho looked at his brother.

"Who the fuck you talking to like that?" Yessy demanded to know.

"My brother. He's laughing at how you're wildin' on me."

"Good! Now tell him that he's gettin' his ass kicked too!"

Macho looked at his brother. "Tamalita's on yo' ass when we get back."

Tool stopped laughing.

Macho started.

"Stop fucking laughing, Antonio!" Yessy shouted.

"I can't, bae! Can you picture bro getting' his ass beat by Tamals? It's hilarious!"

Yessy busted out laughing as she too envisioned the tiny little Belizean beating up the monstrous Steel City Mafia boss.

"That's not funny, yo!" she then said, but was still chuckling.

"Fuck you laughin' for then, punk ass?"

Yessy sighed. "Baby, can you please make sure you and Roberto get back home safely?"

"Claro que sí, mi future wife lady. You know we'll be back."

"How do I know that, Antonio? You are human. Bullets can kill you."

"You know this because... I *am Eeeelll Tiiguurreeee!* Hear me roooaaar!"

Tool laughed his ass off. Yessy screamed out laughing. Even other people eating around them cracked up when they saw Macho acting all theatrical.

"Ay, Dios mío, este hombre 'ta loco, Gabi," Yessy said, laughing so hard she choked. "Bae, I swear to God, I freaking love your wild ass, yo!"

"I love you too, beautiful," Macho replied.

"Me, too, butthead!" Macho heard G-Baby shout out in the background.

"Gabi said she's beatin' your ass too, baby," Yessy made sure he knew.

"Well, at least Tamalita ain't actin' crazy," said Macho.

Tool's iPhone started ringing just then.

"Yet," Macho added, seeing the look on his brother's face that told him who was calling.

"She's calling him right now," Yessy told Macho.

"I know," Macho chuckled, as Tool answered.

"Yes, bae!" Tool said, then put it on speaker.

"Muddafucker! Me *cyant* wait fa ya to bring yo ass back hea'! I'm gonna fuck you up, Roberto!" Macho heard Tamalita snap.

"Tamala," Tool said then.

"What'cha callin' me name for, nigga?"

"I love you, baby," he told her.

No response came.

"She's cheesin' up all hard 'n shit," Yessy told Macho.

Macho laughed.

"Me love ya too, Roberta," Tamalita said, sounding like she was smiling.

"Where are you anyways, Antonio?" Yessy asked.

"The Petro 44 in Joplin."

"Bring me a Philly Cheese Steak N Sub."

"No."

"Fuck you mean no?"

"It's gon' be old 'n cold by the time I get back, Yessy!"

"SO?"

"You're bein' difficult."

"So! Come do somethin' about it!"

"When I get back, *voy a comerte esa chocha bien rico,* y después, *voy a metértelo hasta que venga duuurooo!*"

"Ay, nooo, Antonio! Don't do that when you not here to make it happen, man!" Yessy whined. "Well, stop bein' a butthole or I'ma make yo ass super hot 'n bothered."

"And I'll hang up on you."

"No you won't."

Yessy smacked her lips. "Whatever, mamao. Naw, you know what? *Quieres jugar conmigo?* Okay! Let's play! *Byyeee!*"

She ended the call without another word.

Macho shook his head. He looked at his brother. Tool had the goofiest look on his face as he listened to whatever his lady was saying.

"Bet. Say less, *freca,*" Tool said, then ended his call.

He looked up and saw Macho staring at him with a raised eyebrow.

"A pussy-whipped Waka Flocka Flame-lookin' ass nigga."

Tool laughed. "If I'm Waka, then that makes Tammy mines. Care to come up with something that *isn't* a blessing?"

Their food came just then. The young blonde delivering the meals gave both of them flirty eyes.

"You two enjoy, and if y'all need anything—and I mean *anything* at all—don't hesitate." She walked off, switching her little ass hard. Macho and Tool exchanged glances, then dug into their food.

YESSINIA

The following morning, Michelle pulled up to the house in her super rare two-door convertible Mercedes G50, with her kids in their car seats. Yessy stepped out in a deep-blue silk FeFe top with a black FeFe high-waist skirt, black pumps, and her hair in a bun.

"Yeeessyyy!" Amara screamed excitedly as Michelle took her out of her car seat.

"Heey, pretty lady! I see you, pero, where's my little man?"

"Right here!" Javi Jr. shouted from behind her.

Yessy turned and saw Big Javi's mini there. His hair was in two neat cornrows, the part in between them zigzagged, and the tail bundled at the back of his head. He was dressed in a French Fendi shirt and shorts outfit. Damn—on his feet were little wheat Tims with Fendi F's monogrammed on the tongues. A gold chain hung around his neck, and the gold Patek on his wrist had been resized to fit him. Diamond studs flicked in his ears as well.

"Boy, you are so handsome!" Yessy exclaimed. "And your sister is so *prettyfull!*"

Amara was in Fendi too—little monogrammed shirt with the matching jacket, skirt, and sneakers. Around her neck was a gold necklace, a gold Rolex also resized for her tiny wrist, and on her other wrist was a gold tennis bracelet. Her hair was pulled into two afro puffs. Smiling shyly, Amara hugged her mother's leg. Michelle crouched down and scooped her up, kissing her little angel's face repeatedly, making her giggle.

Yessy couldn't help but smile at the sight of the two. It was such a beautiful thing—for a woman like Michelle to embrace a child who came into the world by her then-boyfriend cheating on her. But the thought of the *disappearance* of Amara's biological mother made her think about Evelyn. Many believed Michelle—the former hitgirl—had offed Angela, who had never been found. But only three people knew the truth: Macho, ChaCha, and Yessy.

"Yo, like, for real, I'm geeked about Kenzie bein' back. She's a dope businesswoman and such a great mother," Yessy acknowledged. "But I can't lie and say that even *I* didn't have the mind to go find her and drag her back by her hair."

Michelle nodded in understanding. "I may have found out where she was and..." Pausing, she sat her daughter down and told her to take her brother toward the mansion's porch. Amara did as she was told. Then, with the kids out of earshot, Michelle continued, "...went to go *encourage* her to make things right."

Yessy narrowed her eyes. "You and ChaCha?" she asked, remembering the call between ChaCha, Macho, herself, and G-Baby, right after exterminating Pancho's crew and snatching him up to send to Africa to meet Heavy B.

Michelle tried not to smile—but failed.

Yessy shook her head. "And is Kenzie living with Xavier again?"

"Yep... and Vanessa, Gianna, Jordan... and Nena."

"Whoa! Mnnn... I am *glad* I will never have to worry about my man and other women pining after him," Yessy said.

Michelle bit her lip to keep what she was thinking to herself, but as she remembered seeing lustful exchanges between a certain two individuals, G-Baby rolled up from her home in her Burnt Oak metallic-colored 2016 Bentley Flying Spur, gliding on 22" Forgiatos. The Bentley was so quiet, despite how powerful the twin-turbo W12 under the hood was. G-Baby's whip was clean and looked amazing—but like every car, truck, and SUV that Macho bought, it was far from normal.

G-Baby hopped out looking fly as ever in a red Valentino dress with a diamond-shaped opening over the tops of her breasts, and a flared mid-thigh hem. Around her waist, a shiny red belt with a gold "V" buckle. The gold pointed-toe 6" Valentino pumps accentuated her toned legs perfectly. Her hair was up in a high ponytail, baby hairs gelled down, enhancing her magnificently beautiful face. The custom gold Audemars Piguet on her wrist shined like the earrings dangling from her ears, and the gold choker around her neck. Her lips matched her dress, eyelids lined with black, and her perfume made her smell like a princess.

"Gaaabiii!" Amara shouted, running toward the Gangsta Boo, excitedly jumping into G-Baby's arms.

"Hiiii, pretty lady!" G-Baby sang out, hugging the little girl as Amara hugged her back. "Awww, Amara, you're so sweet! I know Mr. Javi Jr. better pop up and give me my hug too, though!"

Trying to play it off like he wasn't as excited to see G-Baby as his sister was, Javi Jr. shyly stepped to her. G-Baby scooped him up into her arm, now holding both children.

"Well *daaang*, yo! I need to start workin' out with y'all, B! 'Yahm sayin'?" Michelle chuckled. "I can barely lift one of them up, let alone both."

"You're gonna wanna eat Wheaties before you come work out with us, ma," Yessy said. "We be goin' gorillas."

G-Baby chuckled. "Where you goin' anyways, dressed like you finna go meet the President?"

Wearing a sleek navy-colored sleeveless dress that fit her curvy body perfectly, hem stopping just above her knees, diamond-patterned pantyhose, and 4-inch Jimmy Choos that matched her dress, Michelle was the perfect mix of classy and sexy.

Her hair, like Yessy's, was pulled back into a tight bun, and framing her gorgeous face was a pair of black, nerdy-looking Gucci glasses. From her ears, white gold medallion-like earrings hung; around her neck, a simple white gold necklace; and on her wrists, a white gold Presidential Rolex from the '70s that belonged to her husband.

"Javi and I are headin' out to Calabasas to see a client," Michelle said.

"Eeeeee, Calabasas? You must be about to get a big list of jewelry to make," Yessy guessed.

Michelle looked at the Nuyorican. "Well... not exactly."

Yessy stopped smiling. "Oh... *that.*"

G-Baby knew what *that* was: wet work.

"Someone is tardy on payments and started bumpin' they gums a little too much for me," Michelle explained. "So, Demon's gonna get to have a little fun, 'yah mean?"

"Yes, I do," Yessy nodded. "Just make sure you're back so you can help me kick Antonio's ass."

"Oooooo! Yessy said a bad word, mommy!" Javi Jr. tattled.

Amara started giggling, then said, "Ass!"

"Hey, little girl! Watch your mouth!" Michelle playfully scolded.

Yessy and G-Baby were laughing their asses off at the two little ones.

Javi Jr. and Amara laughed with them.

"Stop teachin' my babies bad words, Yessinia!" Michelle said, full mom-mode.

Yessy stood at attention. "Yes, ma'am! Copy that!"

Michelle muttered, "Ass," under her breath.

"Oooooo! Mommy, you said a bad word!" Javi Jr. pointed out.

"Uh huh. I said a whole *lotta* bad words when ya father and I was creatin' you, so I'm allowed to cuss."

Yessy and G-Baby were rolling in laughter now.

"Yoooo, you're wild!" Yessy laughed, wiping tears from her eyes.

"Anyways, I gots to get goin'." Michelle kissed her daughter, then her son. "Be good for Yessy and Gabi, okay, you two?"

"Yeess!" they shouted in unison.

Michelle hugged Yessy and G-Baby before hopping back into her Benz and pulling off.

"I'm out too, sis," Yessy said. "There's two spare car seats in the auxiliary room in the house."

Yessy hugged the kids, kissed their foreheads, then smacked G-Baby hard on her ass."Ow! You booty hole!" G-Baby screamed, rubbing her hot ass as a laughing Nuyorican ran and hopped into her G-Wagen, peeling off.

The kids were still laughing. G-Baby shook her head, but started laughing too.

"Y'all keep laughin' and we goin' to the shoe store instead of…" She paused and did a drumroll beat. "*Badoom… badoom… boom!* Shedd Aquariiuuuuum!"

"Yaaaaaay!" they both shouted excitedly, then started jumping up and down, chanting, "Shedd! Shedd! Shedd! Shedd!"

G-Baby went and got the car seats and put them in her Bentley. After strapping the kids in, she hopped behind the wheel and started the engine.

"What y'all wanna listen to?" she asked as she pulled off.

Again, in unison, they shouted, "Moneybagg Yooooo!"

G-Baby chuckled, then went into her playlists, selecting one that had the Memphis newcomer's *Heartless* album on it.

Chapter 14

ROMEO

"What's good, ma? How you like workin' with your sister?" Romeo asked.

Returning back to the yard after an overnight run with Anaka, he spotted Mariela pre-tripping her rig before heading out on her maiden voyage as a Numero Uno driver. In her Numero Uno work shirt, tight skinny-leg Diesel jeans, Timberlands, and her long hair in two braids, Romeo couldn't resist going over to try and get some rhythm.

Mariela smiled bashfully, seeing the handsome, thuggish trucker boy again. In his own work clothes, he was fine. A thug and a working man all in one—that's what she liked. That's what she wanted.

"I'm definitely likin' it," she told him. "I wanna make my sister happy—and maybe earn a N.U.T ring while I'm at it."

"Down to Bolingbrook to pick up a couple RV campers, then I'm takin' them up to Zion."

"Oh, okay. You, uh... want some company?" he asked, going for it.

Mariela started smiling again. Her lips parted to respond—but before she could speak, the sound of a truck entering the yard made them both turn to look.

Anaka's T660 was rolling in, pulling a tandem-axle RGN lowboy. From behind the wheel, she stared at him, eyes narrowed like knives.

Romeo caught chills up his spine from the devilish glare.

"I don't think your girlfriend would like that," Mariela told him, locking eyes with Anaka as the Egyptian belle crept toward her parking spot.

"She's not my girlfriend, Mari."

"Oh. Right. Just someone you have sex with and kiss."

Romeo watched G-Baby's sister climb up into her Pete and start her engine.

"You have a good day, Romeo," she said before closing her door.

Standing there, he watched Mariela pull off, heading toward the exit. He smiled to himself, finding now that he had a challenge he was all too willing to meet head on.

"What chu' lookin' at?"

He heard the snap from behind him. Turning, Anaka stood there with her hands on her hips, a scowl on her face.

"Shit," he said.

"Liar! Why you starin' at that bitch like she got something I don't?"

Because she does! Hips, tits, and ass! he thought, but kept that to himself. "You buggin', ma. Ain't nobody thinkin' about her," he said, closing the gap between them. "What I *am* thinkin' about is puttin' it on you again at my new crib... until you cum so hard you go blind."

Anaka started cheesin' at the thought of some good dick. She pulled him by his shirt and looked up at him.

"Talk is cheap, Romeo. Prove it," she said, smiling mischievously now.

"With pleasure," he replied, then ushered her to his Cadillac truck to go handle business.

YESSINIA

Yessy picked Kenzie up from the big eight-bedroom home in Pleasant Prairie that she and her kids now lived in with Xavier, his two other baby mamas, his other children, and the literal zoo of animals he had.

Dressed in office-style attire like Yessy, the redhead was ready for the meeting they were heading to—to buy a two-acre commercial lot from the owner of a business minutes west of Numero Uno's yard. In Kenzie's leather briefcase was the paperwork to close the deal and stacks of cash.

Dani Leigh's *All I Know* featuring Kess bumped as Yessy cruised south, back down Green Bay Road. She re-entered Illinois and minutes later, reached Beach Park.

Waiting in the left-turn lane at the Green Bay and Wadsworth intersection, Yessy saw she needed gas. When the light turned green, she turned onto Wadsworth, then shot a quick right into the Mobil gas station at the corner—across from a Walgreens and a used auto dealership that was also on her list to buy.

Pulling up to a pump, Yessy got out with her wallet. She used her business credit card to purchase premium and began filling her tank.

"Hey! Yessy! Check this out, girl!" Kenzie called out, handing Yessy her iPad through the open window.

Seeing a big listing of commercial properties around Illinois for lease and for sale had Yessy grinning. Many of them were in prime locations for Macho and Tool's expansion plans and sat on acres. As her tank filled, she selected one in Decatur, another in Champaign, and one in East St. Louis.

She handed the iPad back, pulled out her iPhone from her FeFe handbag, and went into her email to check the status of something she was anxious to gift her man. She sent an inquiry to the builder, which got a response in two minutes—with updated photos.

"Oh my God, yo, this thing is *ill,* son! Kenzie! Look, yo!"

Yessy handed the redhead her phone. Kenzie's eyes went wide.

"Daaamn, Yessy! This 'thang is a beast, joe! Is it his birthday or something?"

"Nah. He's always wanted one, so I'ma give it to him," Yessy said as Kenzie gave the phone back.

Just then, Yessy heard a car pull up. Still chatting, she paid it no mind—until she heard a horn beep.

Turning her head, she saw a sleek silver Porsche 918 Spyder parked on the other side of her pump.

Not impressed by the million-dollar Porsche, Yessy turned back to Kenzie—until she heard her name.

"What up, Yessy?"

She turned all the way and saw red immediately when she spotted the almighty Latin King she loathed, getting out of the passenger side.

"Yessy? Isn't that—"

"Yup," said Yessy, cutting Kenzie off. "It's lardass."

Narco chuckled, hearing what she just called him. He raised his hands in surrender, wearing a sarcastic smirk.

Yessy heard another door open and close. She looked past Narco and peeped a woman stepping out from behind the wheel of the Porsche—someone who looked eerily like Chiquis Rivera.

Tall, thick, and buxom, the woman wore a gold leather bodysuit that matched her stilettos and her long golden hair. She was dripping in diamonds, her makeup professionally done.

Yessy looked back at Narco, then quickly reached into her G-Wagen, pulled out her bronze Sig Sauer VM17 from her FeFe bag, and cocked it. She turned, daring him to retaliate for the time she lit his Hellcat's roof up with her drone.

Then she heard the sound of Kenzie's pistol cocking from inside the car.

"Whoa, whoa, whoa. Hold up, Yessy. I don't want no smoke," Narco chuckled.

"Then get the fuck away from me, *gordo!*" Yessy shot back.

"Narco, leave her be, dude!" the woman hollered, peeking around and spotting bystanders now watching the scene—

and cameras everywhere. "Macho's gonna *fuck* you up if he finds out you're screwin' with his lady!"

Narco nodded, then without another word, walked into the store.

Yessy watched him disappear inside and finally let her guard down a bit.

"I'm sorry about him, Yessinia," the woman said.

Yessy looked at her with a frown. "Do I know you?"

"No, but I know you. I'm Nadia, and your man's like a little cousin to me."

"O…Kay. Gotta run," Yessy said, when she realized the nozzle had quit pumping gas into her tank.

"Enjoy your day, Yessy," Nadia said, as the Nuyorican got back in her G-Wagen.

Yessy heard Kenzie groan right as she push-started the engine. "You good?" she asked.

Kenzie shook her head first. "I need a bathroom!"

"There's one inside, Kenzie!"

"Not while they're here! Go…oooo!" She squeezed her legs together as her Crohn's flared up. "To the garage!"

Yessy slammed it in drive and mashed the gas, peeling off in a hurry, before Kenzie had an accident on her exclusive leather seats.

MACHO

Tool was now behind El Viejo's wheel and powered the old Peterbilt back to I-44 to head into Oklahoma.

He took full advantage of the high speed limits. Well-rested from the ride from Joplin, Macho got up from the bed and sat in the passenger seat when Tool hollered to him, letting him know they were a couple miles from the Oklahoma–Texas state line.

Macho popped a mint into his mouth and placed a call to Narco.

"Yeah?" Narco answered, sounding pissed off.

"Fuck wrong with you?" Macho asked him.

"Yo lady upped on me at a gas station twenty minutes ago."

"Word?" Macho stifled a laugh.

"Yeah, bro. Some redhead chick was in her G-Wagen with her, and even she was finna up too!"

"What did you do to them?" wondered Macho, geeked to hear that Kenzie had his woman's back.

"Exist!"

Macho busted out laughing. "Aye, yo, don't worry about them, bro. Is 'ya people on point? We passin' through Shamrock now," he told Narco, looking out the window at the vast desert terrain. "We about 95 miles from Amarillo."

"We?" Narco questioned.

"Yeah. Me and my brother."

"Maaan, bro, you supposed to be dolo, dog!"

Macho got a text from his lady just then. Ignoring Narco for a second, he opened and read it:

Now what! Bet your dick is so hard that it hurts, huh, mamao!

Macho chuckled. The upskirt photos she had sent him were intended to sexually frustrate him, likely to make him go back to her.

"Macho!" Narco hollered.

"Yeah?" Macho answered as he typed a reply:

Nope! HA! Punk ass!

"Why you bring yo brother with you? I don't even know him!"

"I didn't feel like playin' drivin' games by myself." Macho laughed at his own joke.

Yessy replied with a middle finger emoji. Macho sent kissy lips back.

I want you to know that I told ChaCha, Danny, Amir, Perry, AND your grandparents... they're all pissed.

"Maaan, what the fuck, yo?" Macho cursed.

"That's exactly what I was about to say," Narco spoke. "Look, man. When you get there, just post somewhere. My bordermule got hung up in Reynosa for the night."

"You fucking up, fam," Macho said.

Narco chuckled. "Just go get one of them giant-ass steaks from the Big Texan, bro."

"Yup... Love too, 'foo!" Macho clowned.

"Man, shut cho' ass up!"

Macho laughed his ass off as Narco ended the call.

G-BABY

Later that evening...

"¿Qué quieres, cabrón?" she snapped, turning into the Walmart in Zion's parking lot to meet up with Yessy and Kenzie.

"Well damn! What I do to you?" Macho asked.

"You left us! To go down there! For him!"

"You know, when Yessy's mad at me, you are the one that's supposed to make her not mad at me no more."

Seeing Yessy's G-Wagen, G-Baby parked a few spaces down from it. She noticed Romeo's Escalade across from the G-Wagen as she killed the engine.

"Not this time, butthole," said G-Baby, turning around and seeing Javi Jr. and Amara both asleep, tuckered out from a long day of fun down in Chicago. "You gets no love right now, dude!"

Silence. Macho said absolutely nothing.

G-Baby busted out laughing at him.

"Now you finna laugh at me? That's cruel."

"Boy, please. What up, though!"

"Just seein' how your day went with the youngins?"

"All good. We went to Shedd Aquarium, then the museum, and Rainforest Café for lunch," G-Baby told him. "We went to Dave & Buster's out in Vernon Hills, and now we meetin' Yessy and Kenzie at Walmart so we can re-up on stuff for the big dinner we finna make."

"Without me?"

"You are the one that decided to leave, pendejo."

He chuckled. "It's cool. I'm soon to be smashin' on a 72-ounce steak in about an hour and a half."

"Goin' to the Big Texan, huh?" G-Baby guessed.

"YESSIIR!"

"Yessy was gonna pop yo' so-called friend at the gas station by the yard."

"So I heard."

G-Baby put the call on her iPhone and got out, so she could wake the kids up and get them out of their seats. She put her hand on the door handle to open it, when a gold metallic Chevy Caprice big-body slowly rolled up, sitting high up on 30-inch rims.

G-Baby couldn't see the driver through the tinted window, but the rear was rolled down. She locked eyes with Nayeli, the younger sister of Narco, whom—after Yessy had been beat up in a Dominican restaurant owned by Tool—G-Baby had beat up in the bathroom, then stuffed her head in a toilet with pissy water in it.

"Yo, Gabi?" she heard Macho call to her.

"Your little bitch just showed up. I gotta go," G-Baby said, and ended the call before he could respond.

She grabbed her handbag and put it over her shoulder, then, waking the kids up and taking them out of their car seats, she held their hands and ushered them toward the entrance, keeping her eyes on the Donk as it headed toward the other side of the parking lot.

Chapter 15

YESSINIA

She laughed at Kenzie telling her about when she and Nena went toe to toe, after everyone had left the house a few days ago.

"Damn, girl! Is that why she been wearin' them big-ass Chanel shades?" Yessy asked.

Romeo entered the aisle pushing a shopping cart loaded with things on the list Yessy had given him. The look on his face made Yessy furrow up.

"What's wrong with you?" she asked him.

"I think I just saw that dude that Macho fuck with that y'all say a snake, and he with a gang of guys and some females."

G-Baby then turned the corner with Javi Jr. and Amara, looking worried.

"Sis, we need to go! Narco and his sister are here—and some others!"

Then, at the end of the aisle, close to the checkout lanes, Yessy saw him... and his sister, with Nadia and five other guys that were all tatted up with Latin King ink.

"Get behind me, yo," Romeo told G-Baby, grabbing Amara and Javi Jr. to get them by Yessy. Then, locking eyes with Narco, he pulled out the FN Five-Seven he had tucked in his waistline and cocked it.

MACHO

Tool got off of I-40 in Amarillo and made his way toward the big yellow restaurant with a huge bullhead on display.

He reached the entrance to the huge parking lot and turned in, making his way to park in the commercial vehicle lot, finding a spot between a Schneider truck and a USA Truck rig.

As he put the shifter in neutral and put El Viejo's brakes on, Macho got the call he knew was coming—but hoped his phone lost signal before it came.

Tool looked over and saw the hesitance to answer it.

"Answer it, yo."

Sighing, Macho did.

"H-Hello?" he said, as innocently as possible.

"Antonio, ¿qué estás haciendo en Tejas?" boomed the voice of Juanito.

"Um… sooo, I am sittin' in El Viejo, and I'm lookin' at a bull… or a steer… whatever it is."

Tool almost laughed but stopped himself. He knew what was going to happen in 3… 2… 1…

"¡No te pongas pendejo conmigo porque te voy a dar una pata en el culo!"

Macho held his phone away from his ear as his grandfather went ballistic. Tool could hear their grandfather going in on his brother. He felt a sense of relief. If nobody else, when their grandparents got involved, Macho might as well be one of the little kids on the old reality show *Scared Straight*.

"Aight, Grandpa! Dang, man! I'm just helpin' my homeboy out! It's not that big of a deal!"

Suddenly, Macho's door opened up, causing him to nearly fall out of the cab.

In a flash, the .40 caliber Desert Eagle tucked in the left side of the seat was in Macho's hand, pointing outside the door.

"Oh snap," he gasped, seeing his grandfather and his grandmother there. "Now that is just plain scary, yo."

Tool laughed so hard that tears filled his eyes.

"How in the hell are y'all here?" Macho asked, looking around the truck lot but not seeing any Jamaicans.

"My son was killed because he trusted a snake he was warned about!" Carolina snapped. "I will not lose my grandsons to that! Scoot over! We are going home!"

"Maaan, come ooon, Grandma! Can we at least get some steaks before we go?" Macho pleaded.

Carolina paused with a foot up on El Viejo's cab step. She looked at her husband, then the big yellow and blue restaurant.

"Okay," she relented. "Steaks. Then, we are leaving. Give that fat pendejo his money back. Now!"

Macho shook his head but did as told. He hurried to log into his private offshore account on his iPhone and wired back the $15 million Narco paid him upfront. He then sent Narco a text:

Sorry, my boy. Been commandeered by forces that cannot be beaten.

Tool was still laughing his ass off.

"Bro, if you don't stop laughin' at me, we finna kick the fair one in front of all these hick-ass white people."

Tool busted out laughing even harder. Carolina and her husband chuckled while Macho muttered a curse under his breath.

ROMEO

"I'm not lookin' for no trouble," Narco said, taking a few steps forward with his hands raised to show he was peaceful. "I swear it on my crown, but I had to come in here and warn you… there's a mob of Ecuadorians preparin' to run up in here and get it poppin'. They been on one since Pancho disappeared. They know who y'all are."

"We don't know nothin' about no Pancho—and who doesn't know who we are!" Yessy japed.

Screaming and panic erupted suddenly from in front of the store. Yessy grabbed Amara, G-Baby grabbed Javi Jr., and with Kenzie, they took off in the opposite direction of Narco and his posse.

Romeo, however, didn't move.

"Bro! What are you doing? Come on!" Yessy yelled when she realized he hadn't run with them.

Gunshots started flying through the aisle. Items on the shelves exploded as bullets hit them. Romeo ducked down, narrowly missing taking a slug to the dome.

Narco and his people upped the pistols they all came in with and started firing back.

"Rome!" G-Baby shouted.

"Go! Get the kids to safety!" he yelled back, just as Nayeli screamed in pain when a slug hit her in the shoulder.

Romeo hopped up and ran toward the action and saw more than twenty Latinos had run up in the Walmart, all of them blowing down any and everyone that hadn't come with them.

Raising his FN up, he took aim at one of the men, ready to pop him—when he felt cold steel touch the back of his head and heard someone laughing behind him.

MACHO

"What! Yeah! Y'all see that?" shouted Macho, holding up the big bare bone of the enormous steak he had just smashed in record time, beating the last guy's record. His steak was now free.

"Beat that, goddammit! Woooo!"

Tool, Juanito, and Carolina laughed at Macho doing the "Swole Man" dance, kissing his big biceps as he danced.

A number of women in the shanty-style restaurant were mesmerized by the handsome city slicker, including some of the waitresses.

"Hey there, sugar," a busty blonde chick in a waitress uniform said, standing next to him, her breasts threatening to spill out of her shirt. "I make a mean country-fried steak and eggs. Ya wanna come home with me?" she asked, damn near purring sex.

"Whooaa… no," he told her. "My woman would dismember you, ma."

"¡Puta, muévete!" Carolina snapped, getting on the woman's ass. "He has a woman!"

The lady backed away, not wanting to lock horns with the crazy ol' lady—nor lose her tip.

Juanito took his wallet, filled with C-notes. He dropped two $100s on the table.

"Let's go, boys. We've had our steaks, fun, and now it's time to go," he said.

"Lemme use the bathroom real fast, ol' man," Macho said, then hurried off to go drain his bladder.

"Aawww yeeeaaah! Woo!" Macho shouted as he took a long piss.

When he was empty, he went to wash his hands. As he lathered them with soap, the door flew open and smacked the wall. He jumped from the loud BAM! and saw two Hispanic men rush in—wearing cowboy hats, flannel shirts, jeans, cowboy boots—and they both had pistols in their hands.

"Uh… I guess y'all aren't here for the steak," Macho said.

Then…

BOC! BOC! BOC! BOC! BOC! BOC! BOC! BOC! BOC! BOC! BOC! BOC!

ROMEO

"Die, pussy!" he heard a man snarl behind him.

He closed his eyes, the sounds of gunshots fading as he retreated into the deepest parts of his mind. He said his prayers and asked God to let his family make it out—before he asked the Man to open those gates for him.

CRACK!

"AGN!"

Romeo heard the sound of a skull cracking and a yelp, then a thump.

"Aye, man? Fuck is you standin' there for?"

He looked up and saw Narco there, gripping a big Desert Eagle.

BOOM! BOOM! BOOM! BOOM!

He blew the man that had been seconds away from ending Romeo's life to hell.

Narco's guys were locked in, shooting it out with the mob of Ecuadorians. Bullets flew, people dropped, screams wailed out. Pandemonium erupted as more shooters ran into the store with only one thing on their minds: murder.

"Go get yo' sister 'n 'nem up outta here!" Narco shouted, and ran to where his cousin was pressing a shirt over the gunshot wound in her shoulder while they ducked for cover.

Romeo took off to go find Yessy, the kids, and the others. He nearly collided with G-Baby as she rounded the end of the aisle.

"Come on!" she shouted, with a fully automatic Glock 18 in her hand, equipped with a 30-round clip.

Romeo glanced back once more, just as he saw Narco and his Chiquis Rivera-clone cousin trying to get Nayeli up so they could get up out of there.

A man with an AK ran around the corner and pointed the chopper at them.

BOC! BOC! BOC! BOC! BOC!

Romeo fired at the man, hitting him dead in the face, saving the three from sure death.

Realizing what he'd just done, Narco looked up at him and nodded in appreciation, then yelled for him to get gone.

He followed G-Baby to where Yessy, the kids, and Kenzie were in the rear stocking room area. But the second they entered, they saw another mob of Ecuadorians with choppers, holding them all at gunpoint.

"Drop them guns!" one demanded, pointing his AK at Romeo, while another was aiming at G-Baby.

"Chill, yo. We droppin' 'em," Romeo said, glancing at his sister.

Yessy stood in front of Javi Jr. and Amara, prepared to use her body as a shield. Kenzie, terrified, stood next to Yessy. Though she was scared shitless, she was prepared to die to save the kids.

Javi Jr. held his sister's hand, keeping her behind him out of pure instinct. He was young, but since learning how to talk and understand words, one thing his father had made sure he never forgot was to always be there for his little sister.

"Where's Macho?" the man asked them all. "Give him up, and you all walk out of here!"

Yessy started laughing the second a beeping sound came.

The Ecuadorian that had spoke frowned. He pointed his gun at her face.

"Did I say something funny, bitch?"

"Yeah, you did, but I'm not laughing at 'ya clown-ass, pendejo," Yessy said. "I'm laughing at what your face is gonna look like when you go meet Sleezy."

Romeo's brows furrowed. He glanced over at G-Baby and saw that she was smirking. Kenzie looked puzzled and the kids looked determined.

"Sleezy these buts, bitch! I'm gonna shoot yo fuckin' face off!" the man growled and wrapped his finger around the trigger.

BOOM!

An explosion from above blew a gaping hole in the ceiling. The Ecuadorians all immediately pointed their guns up to blast whomever came through it.

BOOM!

Another explosion blew a massive hole in the rear wall, then the door to the store area was blown to pieces.

From three directions, Romeo saw that help had arrived. He was beyond shocked when he saw big guns pointing through the hole in the roof, as a mob of masked gunners ran in through the hole in the wall.

The Ecuadorians were overtaken in mere seconds. The mob of Jamaicans that ran in through the hole were armed with .50 caliber machine guns. Up on the roof, pointing H&K G36s through the hole made by breach charges, were Chloe, Stella, and Bella, along with the giant braided-up twins Shane and Mane, and Nya.

At the hole where the door used to be: Anaka, Lauren, Tati, Maria, Simone, Tiffany, Brittany, Analise, DeeDee, Perla, Victoria—all armed with fully automatic H&Ks with 100-round drums and red beams.

The lead Ecuadorian was beyond tripping.

Then, through the mob of ladies, ChaCha, followed by DBoy, stepped through. They both had bloody machetes in their right hands, and in their lefts, the severed heads of two Ecuadorian shooters.

YESSINIA

"Take the kids," she told Kenzie. "Go with Jamaica; we'll handle this."

Nodding, Kenzie took the kids by their hands and hurried to where the head Rasta—best friend of Macho's great-uncle Diego, the leader of the Valdez family's Caribbean army—waited. Jamaica and his right hand, Gold Mouth, ushered the redhead and the kids out of the danger zone.

Yessy stepped up to the man in charge. She took his gun, looked at it, then had her crew disarm the others.

"Now, you should already be very sure that your friends are dead, and you all that are right here are fucked," Yessy said to him as he trembled in fear. "Unless!" she continued, glancing over at ChaCha and DBoy.

"Vito!" the guy snitched, quicker than Yessy anticipated. "We just do our job, shortie! That's all!"

WHAM! With lightning-fast speed, Yessy bashed him in his jaw with the butt of his chopper, knocking him right out! ChaCha and DBoy dropped the severed heads and walked up to two others.

"No, no, no, wait!" one pleaded.

THWACK! DBoy swung his machete and sliced right through the middle of the guy's face, taking everything from his eyes and up completely off.

ChaCha hurled her machete at the one in her line of sight who tried to get away. The machete sailed right into his back, hitting his spine, paralyzing him from the legs down.

Still able to move his upper body, he tried to crawl away.

A pair of Timberlands appeared in front of him. He looked up and saw a bulky dark-skinned man with a fresh bold fade haircut, pointing two Glock .40s at his face.

BOC! BOC! BOC!

BOC! BOC! BOC!

Xavier stared at the headless shooter for a minute, then looked up as Yessy came to his side.

"Time to go," she said, bringing him out of the enraged state he'd flown into when he got the call from G-Baby, anticipating something very bad popping off when she saw Nayeli.

She'd called Yessy as well, all the while sending a group text to the Numero Uno, knowing that nobody was working—since she hadn't booked any of them loads to pick up—to get to the Walmart ASAP and be ready for battle.

Rushing out of the rear stock area, a line of Sprinter vans and Hummer H2s awaited. Everyone hopped into the vehicles, except for Yessy, G-Baby, ChaCha, and DBoy. Yessy and G-Baby stood next to each other, holding the AK-47s of two dead shooters.

"Cierra los ojos," G-Baby told them.

The Ecuadorians closed their eyes and prepared to die.

"Rest in piss, pussies!" Yessy then shouted.

She and G-Baby squeezed the triggers and swept left and right. In seconds, the last of the mob were turned into piles of bloody meat and bone.

"Alrighty, then, Gabi Poo. Let's ride," Yessy said. Then, keeping the choppers, she and G-Baby hurried with ChaCha and DBoy to where DBoy's Avalanche was parked.

Chapter 16

MACHO

Then gunshots filled the bathroom, ricocheting off the walls. He heard them clearly, but didn't feel pain.

He could hear his own breath, and his heart beating, fast. His blood pumped coldness throughout his entire body. His eyes, frozen, looking at the sight in front of him. He could not believe what he was seeing.

They were dead. Both of them. Blood poured through the holes that bullets had riddled them with. One of them—the top of his head was gone, and his brain was splattered on the wall next to him.

Screaming, crying, and more gunshots came from outside of the bathroom; he couldn't make his feet move, despite the urge to go find his grandparents and his brother.

BRRRRRRR! BRRRRRRRR! BRRRRRR!

He heard more gunshots from assault rifles, and more screaming.

"¡Antonio! ¿Estás bien?" she asked.

He couldn't find his voice to respond. Seconds later, Carolina rushed in, holding two Sig Sauer 9mm pistols.

"¿¡Qué haces? ¡Necesitamos irnos ahora mismo!" his grandmother told him urgently. "¡VAMOS!"

Macho managed to move one foot, then the other. Before he knew it, he'd made it to where the two dead sicarios lay.

"Come on, papacito!" Carolina shouted again, as the shooting continued but the screaming ceased.

Macho reached down and grabbed both of the automatic Uzis. With 50-round clips sticking out, fully loaded, he realized the two sicarios had come to light him up.

"Mamahuevos," he grumbled at them. Then, looking at his grandma, he nodded his head. "Let's ride, ol' lady!"

BOC! BOC! BOC! BOC! BOC! BOC! BOC!

BOCKA! BOCKA! BOCKA! BOCKA! BOCKA!

Tool and Juanito fired repeatedly at the three shooters taking cover by an old vintage wooden wagon-styled dinner table. The shooters fired their choppers back as the two used a thick wooden table as cover for themselves.

The bodies of customers that'd come to enjoy a delicious western meal lay scattered around the dining area. Blood pooled all over the floor. A fire started by bullets hitting lights and other electrical equipment was quickly growing into a raging inferno. The restaurant was filled with thick smoke, making it so much harder to see.

Where the fuck are they? Tool asked himself, praying that his grandmother and brother would appear unharmed.

"¡Te vamos a matar, pinche puto!" he heard one of the shooters shout.

The guy hopped up from his spot and ran toward the flipped-over table, squeezing the trigger of his AR. He fired round after round as he advanced.

The table split into two as the 5.56 NATO rounds finally penetrated the super thick oakwood.

He kicked one piece away and pointed at where the two had been ducking... but they weren't there.

"What the—"

BOC! BOC! BOC! BOC! BOC!

Tool hopped up from under the table next to where he and his grandfather had been and popped the shooter in the chest and face.

"Motherfuuucheerr!" yelled one of the other two that remained, jumping up and taking aim at Tool.

Juanito appeared at the man's side and put the barrel of his .45 to the shooter's temple.

BOCKA!

One to the dome blew his brains out.

The last shooter jumped up but didn't shoot. He dropped his gun and held his hands up.

"Por favor, ¡no me mates!" he begged, pleading for his life.

BRRRRRRR!

BRRRRRRR!

The shooter's chest opened up as a barrage of bullets slammed into him. He flew back into a wall, then slid down to the floor, leaving a bloody trail behind him.

"Bro! Viejo!" Tool then heard, and sighed in relief.

He and Juanito saw the wildcard of the family, leading Carolina from where she'd gone to rescue him.

MACHO

"Yo, ya'll good?" Macho shouted, barely able to see through the fire and smoke.

"Yeah!" he heard his brother shout back, choking from lungfuls of smoke. "We gotta go! Come on!"

Taking his grandmother's hand, Macho led her through the smoke toward where he remembered the exit was. Making it outside, he saw his brother and grandfather were disheveled—but good.

The sounds of engines gunning came. They looked and saw four county sheriff pickup trucks speeding up. Macho and Tool took aim at them, ready to blast their way out of the Big Texan, when suddenly, one exploded, then another, then the third.

"What the fuck?" Macho said, baffled.

The fourth sheriff pickup tried to turn around and dip, but the driver's efforts were futile.

A rocket flew right through the windshield and exploded, frying the two officials inside.

Macho looked into a nearby field and saw a motorcade of SUVs and pickup trucks, parked a few hundred feet away from the restaurant's main parking area, looking like something out of the movie *Mad Max*.

"These muhfuckaz got rocket launchers, yo," Macho said, seeing a man holding an RPG while the others had choppers.

"That means we should go now!" Tool said.

"¡Dale! We'll catch up!" Juanito told them.

He and his wife ran off in the opposite direction as gunshots started flying at them.

Macho and his brother ran toward where El Viejo was, firing back. They made it by the skin of their teeth. Tool jumped up behind the wheel and started the engine. Macho kept shouting at the sicarios until the Uzis clicked empty, then he hopped up into the passenger side.

"Hold on to 'ya ass, lil bro! Wood!" Tool shouted, releasing the brakes, slamming it into 3rd, and hitting it.

The Caterpillar roared, turbos whistling, as Tool put the pedal to the metal and speed-shifted gears like the pro that he was. Making it away from the fiery carnage that was now swarmed with cops and state troopers, Tool made it to U.S. Highway 60, then he hurried to get eastbound.

In the passenger seat, Macho had the old school SK that had its own secret spot up in the ceiling. He took the 30-round banana clip loaded with 7.62s and locked it in, readying it for the next round.

"Here they come, bro!" Tool hollered over the loud engine roaring out of the straight stacks.

Macho looked in the passenger side mirror and counted at least eight vehicles.

"Okay, then. Gonna need something bigger than this," he said, then reached over to the Kenwood pop-out head unit and turned the music up.

Westside Connection's *Bow Down* started playing. Tool busted out laughing as his brother got up and went back into the sleeper, hitting a secret button and unlocking the base of the bed to retrieve the mighty street sweeper that was tucked in the custom-made gun rack.

"¡Ándale, ándale, ándale! ¡Mátalos, esos putas madres!" Checko shouted into his radio to his team.

The murderous Mexican mercenaries had come up from Matamoros to execute the Dominican cocaine lord and collect the massive bounty placed on his head.

With fourteen vehicles filled with killers, Checko had come prepared. He was well aware of all the failed attempts made to get the target—and even ones made on other members of the family. He had absolutely no plans on going back to Mexico without the man that had taken out Macho Valdez.

In the middle of his motorcade, Checko held onto his MP5. The two men in the back had MP5s as well. The Wranglers in front of the Ford F-250 that he was in contained the RPG.

The vehicles in front of him broke formation to get to it. Four swerved into the two oncoming lanes, the fifth got in the hammer lane, and the Wrangler stayed in front of Checko's pickup, in the granny lane.

The man smirked as his men—hanging out of the windows and standing through sunroofs, others standing up in the beds of pickups—started shooting at the back of the old Peterbilt's box-shaped sleeper, some of them aiming at the window in the center of it.

Behind the wheel of the F-250, Ruben's eyebrows furrowed when he saw that not a single bullet had penetrated the sleeper.

"¡Híjole de la chingada, güey! The *pinche troca* is armored, jefe!" he exclaimed, shocked by the fact that he'd never known anyone to make a semi-truck bulletproof.

Checko cursed. He heard his men call to him and ask what the heck to do now.

"Fire the RPG!" he told the men in the Wranglers. "Blow them off the road, then we—"

An explosion behind him halted Checko's words. He and Ruben looked in their mirrors and saw a huge ball of fire shooting up to the sky that had come from one of his vehicles bringing up the rear.

"¿Que chingao? Another one?" Ruben gasped, seeing another ol' school behind the crew, doing a lot of damage.

MACHO

"Uh oh! Uh oh! ¡Juanito y carolina están aquí, Tiguere!" shouted Macho, looking out the rear window in El Viejo's sleeper.

He could just make out his grandmother hanging out the window, blasting at the Jeep in front of Juanito's classic 1984 GMC 5-Star General with an assault rifle. She blew the vehicle's rear window out, then hit a button on her weapon and shot a grenade inside of it.

BOOM! The Jeep exploded with such a blast that it went airborne. Juanito smacked into it with his silver bullet semi, sending it flying off the road.

Macho saw his grandma start shooting at another Jeep.

"I see you, ol' lady! I got chu, yo!" he shouted with a grin.

As KRS-One's *"Step Into a World (Rapture's Delight)"* pounded—one of Macho's favorite cuts—he unlocked the bunk bed, lifted it, and raised up the deadly automatic M134 GAU/17 that Tool mounted in for extreme measures. Macho equipped the 500-round belt of 7.62-millimeter rounds, opened the sleeper's rear window, and pointed the new-age gatling gun at the mercenaries.

"Okay! Okay! You wanna play? Okay! Let's play, mama huevos!" he shouted, then squeezed the trigger and made it rain on them.

"Holy shit! Ruben, get us outta here!" Checko yelled, as the deadly spitter took out the vehicles in front of him, while the old woman in the GMC semi behind them scattered the others.

Ruben swerved hard to the left, seconds before blood and guts from the man standing through the roof of the Wrangler—holding the RPG—flew onto the F-250's windshield when swarms of NATO rounds hit him.

The old pickup started sliding more than Ruben meant for. He tried to countersteer to straighten it back up. Checko was in his ear, cursing him out, demanding he hurry up and get them out of there.

"¡Jefeee! ¡Gooo!" one of the guys in the backseat yelled in terror.

Checko and Ruben turned their heads to the left, looking out of the driver-side window, as the pickup came to a stop in the middle of the two eastbound lanes.

"Fuck me," Checko cursed, then closed his eyes…

MACHO

"3!... 2!... 1!..." he counted down excitedly.

BOOM!

"Wooooo! Yippie-ki-yay, muthafuckaaaa!" Macho shouted, as Juanito T-boned the old Ford F-250 pickup truck so hard that it exploded and split in two.

The General blew through the pickup, virtually unscathed. He turned the music down and heard his grandpa's voice.

"¡Nietos! Go to the duck-off ahora!" Juanito commanded.

Macho sat back in his seat. "Maaaan… I should call 50 Cent and have him make a movie outta this shit, yo! Homiez! Er'body would be like *Power* what?"

Tool chuckled. "Let's see if you still all geeked up when Yessy learns about this," he said. "And G-Baby. And Eve. And Michelle. And ChaCha."

"Good thing we gotta go underground for a few days," Macho said as Tool came up on the exit for Hemphill. "By then, they'll all be cool and won't get to trippin'."

Tool busted out laughing. "Keep tellin' yourself that, lil bro."

Chapter 17

YESSINIA

"What?"

She knew he was going to be pissed. The anger in his voice damn near blew the speakers inside DBoy's Avalanche as he turned into the driveway behind the others.

"Baby, please, calm down!" Yessy begged. "We are okay! Everyone is fine!"

G-Baby was still rattled by it all. It was one thing to be in an intense shootout, but to have such young children to protect while staying alive was enough to shake anybody.

"Yessinia, when y'all get home, do not leave! Swear to God I am not playing! You! Rome! Gab! Stay there!"

"Okay, Antonio! Damn, get off the gas pedal, yo!"

ChaCha, DBoy, and G-Baby remained quiet as DBoy entered the gates. They heard Macho speaking to someone—likely it was Tool.

"I'm sorry, baby. I'm heated though, yo! You and Gabi are my world! Romeo's my lil' mans, ya mean! I'd go crazy if someone took y'all from me!"

Tears rolled down Yessy's face as she recounted the events. A simple trip to the store turned into the deadliest gun battle she'd ever been in—even in her time in the Army.

What really screwed with her head was seeing, with her own eyes, Narco saving her brother's life. She'd been about to turn the corner out of the aisle when she saw one of the shooters creep up behind him and put a gun to the back of his head. When she saw Narco crack the guy in the back of his head with his pistol, then blast him, she was so shocked she couldn't even move her feet. Kenzie and G-Baby had brought her out of her stupor, then got her and the kids into the back.

"Where's Mari at?" she heard Macho ask, just as Yessy came back from the trip down nightmare lane. "And ya girl Esmeralda?"

"They're at home. They finished their route an hour before we went to the store."

DBoy went around the other vehicles and parked at the front of the mansion.

"Tell everybody to go home," Yessy told G-Baby.

Getting out, G-Baby dismissed everyone, telling them to keep their eyes open. Xavier offered to take his niece and nephew with him and Kenzie. Yessy didn't want to let Amara and Javi Jr. out of her sight any time soon. Xavier understood, then got back in the H2 with Kenzie and was chauffeured off.

Yessy told Macho about Narco's deed, and waited for it.

"See? I told you he a good dude. Can you stop hating on him now, please? And his sister?"

Yessy groaned. "Uh-huh. When are you coming home, bae? I really need you."

"Gotta stay low for a while, amor. We just stirred up a lot of shit. Good thing ol' girl is outta the picture."

"You sound real confident about that."

"Believe me, baby… she will not be fucking with us anymore," Macho told her.

Yessy sighed. "I love you, baby."

"I love you too, beautiful... Stay in the house!"

***

Yo, on everything I love, it's on and poppin' when we get back, son! ¡Esos hijos de la gran putas van a morir por jodiendo con mis pequeños! ¡Te lo fucking prometo!

Yessy read the text that had just come from Michelle, replying to her message informing the Dominicana of what had gone down. She knew Michelle had a wrath like no other. The woman knew how to inflict the most excruciating pain and death.

Responding back, Yessy apologized profusely. She felt horrible and knew that even the cop connections they had might not cover them for the bloodbath they'd washed the shooters up in.

Waiting outside with Romeo, G-Baby, and the kids, Yessy saw the headlights of her G-Wagen, G-Baby's Bentley, and Romeo's Escalade as they each turned onto the street. She was relieved that the Rastas had retrieved their vehicles from the Walmart.

As the three came to a stop in front of where they stood, Yessy ran to the rear passenger door and opened it, as a Hummer H2 came up and parked.

Dreams and Maliante jumped right out, still on edge from their canine detection skills sensing she was in trouble—even from inside the G-Wagen where she'd temporarily left them while she and Kenzie and the kids went into the store.

They were shaking. Not in fear, but relieved to see their human was safe. Yessy patted them both down as they licked her face, grunting and snorting happily. G-Baby and the kids walked up and got some of that wild dog love canines were well known to give when trying to cheer their people up.

Romeo stayed where he was and watched the two dreadheads hop out of the G-Wagen, while four others got out of G-Baby's Flying Spur and Rome's Escalade.

From Yessy's G-Wagen, Shabba got out from behind the wheel, along with Gold Mouth out of the passenger's side. Shabba was a tall, wiry man with skin the color of Kingsford charcoal. Gold Mouth was just as dark and had the shiniest golds in his mouth. He was tall and thin as well, both of them in their late 40s.

Face and Sticks got out of G-Baby's Bentley, both lighter in skin tone than the first two, but still dark, and only in their mid-30s. The two that got out of Romeo's Escalade were West and Pep. Like their other four Rasta brothers, they were dark-skinned, in their later years, tall and skinny with long dreads.

"Thank you, Shabba," Yessy said to the man in charge of the five others. "We're good now. You all can go."

Shabba looked at her with reluctance in his eyes. "Ya know me 'cyant leave ya, Yessy. Tonio would have me head."

"No he won't. You do remember this entire subdivision is filled with ex-military, dope dealers, and killers? When's the last time you heard of anybody living here dealing with break-ins or trespassers?"

"Ya, mon. 'De queen o' de castle no wan' standby eyes here, neph."

Yessy instantly knew he had called Macho.

Shabba looked at Yessy and G-Baby, then ended the call. "Man say—"

"Don't leave the house!" they mocked together.

"We know, Shabba," Yessy said. "Sorry to be snappy, but I'm pissed."

"Me undastand, gal. Ya need us, ya call, ya war me?" Shabba asked.

Yessy nodded. "My wood, yo. Thank you. All of you."

The dreads nodded their heads. Shabba gave her a reassuring hug, then the six Rasta goons hopped into the Hummer H2 and left, but had no intentions at all of going too far.

Yessy giggled and squealed as Macho nibbled on her earlobe. "Baaee, no, come on! Stooop!" she playfully whined.

He chuckled deeply, which got her hotter than she already was. "You know you don't want me to stop, punk," he told her, then started kissing on her neck.

"Yes, I do want you to stop, Antonio," Yessy said, but then, grabbing the collar of his shirt, she pulled his face to hers. "I want you to stop talking, and fuck me so good that when I cum, we both look like we went swimming."

"Daayum!" he busted out laughing. "I can definitely make that happen, baby."

He pulled her over the center console, onto his lap, so that she was straddling him. Yessy reached behind her and turned the music up. Rick Ross's "YOU THE BOSS," featuring Nicki Minaj, was on and bumping from the stock, hot superb audio system in the exclusive drop-top Rolls-Royce Dawn.

Macho reached his hands around her rear end, raising her tiny leather-pleated skirt. He palmed her phat juicy 46" ass as she pulled her long-sleeved belly top off, revealing no bra covering her succulent 36DD cups.

He leaned forward, kissing her chest before taking her left breast into his mouth. Yessy moaned, gasping as she threw her head back from the feeling of his tongue swirling around her nipple. She cried his name out in straight bliss.

"Ay, mi amor! Me encanta, papi! I love it!" she shouted.

Reaching down under her, Yessy worked his bone-hard cock free of his jeans. While he continued sucking her breast, she lifted up, slid her tiny lace thong to the side, and slid down on his length.

"Oooo shit, that thang so juicy!" Macho exclaimed, loving how warm, wet, and tight the pussy was. "Damn, esa chocha, fresca! Dámela, mami!"

She started grinding on him, getting all of him inside her. The bliss she felt whenever they became one was like giving herself to him for the first time. It was magical. It was hot and so fulfilling that she always felt like she would spontaneously combust, just off of his touch.

Lil Durk's "LIKE ME," featuring Jeremih, came on as they continued getting wild in the all-white and woodgrain interior of the half-million-dollar 2-door.

Yessy started trembling minutes later. She felt it coming—strong. She sped up, bouncing up and down on him like he was her pogo stick.

Macho's eyes rolled to the back of his head as she worked him. She was going crazy, getting all of him, as if there'd be no more when they were done.

He reached behind her again, groaning, cursing, his pleasure peaking like they were fucking at the opening of an active volcano. He grabbed her juicy booty cheeks again, squeezing them, smacking them. He loved how plump and soft it was. He couldn't resist caressing his woman's ass every chance he got.

He cursed out loud as Yessy went even harder on him. He kept on squeezing and rubbing on her ass, in love with it.

Then he brought his right hand up to her mouth. Yessy took his middle finger in, sucked on it, made it wet, then spit it out. Macho then stuck it into her asshole, making Yessy squeal out in delight.

Lil Durk's *Rider Chick* featuring Dej Loaf, came on just then. They turned up; he turned her around so she could ride his dick reverse cowgirl.

Macho's dick got even harder inside her as he watched that big caramel ass bounce while Yessy gripped the leather and wood steering wheel.

"Woo! Fuck!" he shouted out.

Yessy screamed even louder as she got close to climaxing.

"Aaayyy, shhiiiit! Papi! Me vengo! Me vengo! Ohh God!"

Seconds later, Yessy exploded, cumming all over his dick. Macho then busted his nut, cumming inside her. Yessy kept riding him, working her pussy muscles, making her tight walls grip his rock until he was empty.

"Holy shit! Goddamn, bae," Macho exclaimed, feeling winded.

Yessy leaned in and started kissing him so wildly that he damn near thought she would eat his lips.

"Um… ma'am… sir?"

Yessy paused and at the same exact time, she and Macho looked and saw the girl wearing a Hillery's uniform, standing next to the car with a tray loaded with their delicious barbecue ribs, macaroni and cheese, and french fries.

The young African-American woman's eyes displayed sheer shock. Yessy looked around the parking lot of the popular barbecue joint in Waukegan and saw a few other couples in the lot—all of them with wide eyes and dropped jaws. She heard a female shout, "You go girl! Ain't nothin' wrong with fuckin' in public!"

Then another one shouted, "Especially when you 'bout to eat some fi' ass ribs!"

Yessy and Macho busted out laughing, as did the employee chick.

BOCKA! BOCKA! BOCKA! BOCKA!

In the blink of an eye, the girl's brains were all over Yessy and Macho. The couples in the lot screamed from the gunshots hitting the girl, blowing her head off.

Stuck in shock from the lightning-fast change of events, Yessy and Macho looked out into the middle of the lot as the others ran off screaming in panic.

"Y'all muthafuckas thought it was sweet?" yelled Narco, then raised up his twin semi-autos. "I got y'all now, muthafuckas!"

Yessy hit the button on the side of the seat and made it drop low as more gunshots came. Macho was frozen in place, not blinking, like he was just a shell.

"It's okay! I got us, baby!" Yessy told him, reaching down on the side of the seat to grab the ARP Macho had tucked between it.

Bullets hit the car but didn't penetrate. Yessy heard Narco shout, "Stop hidin'! I thought you was a gangsta, Macho! You's a bitch!"

BOCKA! BOCKA! BOCKA! BOCKA! BOCKA!

"This punk fuckin' mamabicho got me all the way fucked up, yo!" Yessy said, then she shot up and got ready to take him out with the mini AR-15.

But he was gone...

"Pssst! Lookin' for me?"

Yessy whipped her head around toward the passenger's side and saw him there, the two Glocks pointed right at her.

Narco smirked and winked at her. "It's been real, shorty."

"Nooo!"

BOCKA! BOCKA! BOCKA! BOCKA!

"Aaaaaaaaaaaaaaaaaaahhhhhhhhhhhhhhhhh!"

BOOM BOOM BOOM BOOM BOOM BOOM BOOM!

Yessy squeezed the trigger over and over until half of the 30-round clip was empty. She blinked and realized she hadn't shot Narco, but the big wall-sized 4K HDTV in her and Macho's expansive master bedroom.

Amara and Javi Jr. screamed in fear from the gunshots waking them up out of their sleep. The dogs ran in expecting to take someone down but only saw Yessy holding a smoking Desert Eagle.

Romeo then ran in with an AK, with G-Baby right behind him, clutching an H&K G36.

"Oh my God!" Yessy dropped the gun and went for the kids, pulling them into her arms. "Shhh… it's okay! It's okay! I'm sorry! I'm so sorry!"

"What happened?" Romeo asked, looking around the dimly lit room, with the chopper aimed and ready to spit.

"It was… it was a dream… a nightmare," Yessy admitted, cradling the two-year-olds, rocking them back and forth.

"Are you okay?" G-Baby asked, stepping up to her side.

"No! I want Antonio here! I need him here with me, Gabi!" Yessy said, her voice breaking, eyes filling with tears.

G-Baby set her automatic down and threw her arms around Yessy, hugging her tightly as the kids began to calm down.

Romeo sighed in relief. He was glad that nothing was wrong—more than what was already going on—but he couldn't help hoping that Macho and Tool would be back very soon.

Chapter 18

The following morning, Yessy sent a text to her man:

I am not missing this business meeting, Antonio. I know you don't want me to leave the house, but I have to be there! I will be careful, but I'm not tucking my tail and hiding from nobody!

Already dressed in a simple blue silk blouse, beige leggings, and beige pumps, Yessy wasn't trying to hear anything other than "Okay. Love you!"

Dreads go with you. No ifs, ands or buts," Macho replied.

Yessy groaned.

Take it or stay home, another reply came seconds later.

Yessy agreed. Then, after putting her hair up in a tight bun, she grabbed her two new Glock 18s—both rare, fully automatics—with six extra 30-round clips of hollow points on top of the two already locked in, and put them in her mini New York Knicks duffel bag. She added her backup Desert Eagle, also with extended clips full of .40 caliber rounds.

Downstairs, Yessy reached the bottom step just as G-Baby opened the door for Michelle and Javi. The two ran in, right to where their son and daughter were in the living room, watching cartoons with the dogs.

"Mommy! Daddy!" they both yelled with excitement.

"Ay, my babies!" Michelle cooed, hugging both at the same time and kissing their faces, never wanting to let them out of her sight again. "Mommy and Daddy are here! Are y'all okay?"

"Yes!" they said.

"I protected Amara, Mommy!" Javi Jr. said proudly.

"Good job, baby! I'm proud of you, baby boy!"

"Me too, lil dude," Javi said, then dapped his little man up.

Javi looked at Yessy and G-Baby. "Y'all okay?"

They nodded, but it wasn't convincing.

Michelle kissed her babies again, then rose up and hugged Yessy and G-Baby, tearing up as her emotions threatened to break loose.

"Swear to God, I can't even explain how grateful I am for y'all keepin' them safe, yo. Thank y'all so much," Javi told the puertorriqueñas.

"Somos familia," G-Baby replied.

"Where's Rome?" Michelle asked, noticing the young buck was nowhere to be seen.

"In his room, still knocked out," Yessy told her. "I have a business meeting to go to. The four-and-a-half-acre dirt lot is for sale out in Libertyville, right on Milwaukee Ave before you get into Vernon Hills. I can buy it cheap, develop it for someone to build on, then sell high."

"While you're trying to shake Jamaica's guys," Javi said with a knowing smile.

Yessy denied it at first. They twisted their lips at her.

"Okay, whatever. Hush!" she fired off like that famous sassy Nuyorican type. "I don't need a babysitter, though!" She held up her Knicks bag. "Believe me, I do not!"

"Oh we know this, Yessinia," said Michelle. "But just humor him, ma. You know his main worry is your safety. Truth be told, anybody can fall when they're dolo. There is strength in numbers."

"Real talk," Javi agreed.

"Fiiiine!" Yessy groaned. "I need to go."

She hugged everyone, kissed Maliante on his nose, then Dreams, before leaving out of the house to hop into her G-Wagen.

ROMEO

Four days later...

He smiled at the sight of his bank account via the banking app on his iPhone. Since he'd left selling pounds of high-grade weed alone and got into trucking with his sister, Romeo had seen a significant rise in his money. He'd really only been trucking loads with his Coronado and had already amassed just over $15,000. He hadn't had to stay out on the road for more than two days—not that he'd have cared if it came to that.

The mini-gangsta Boo had been putting some serious miles on her truck, clocking major hours. She was a real driver—one that didn't want to get off the road. He had a lot of respect and admiration for Mariela. Hell, any woman that was getting it on her own and not depending on some clown to take care of them.

Yessy walked out of the tall building just after six in the evening, with her leather satchel in her hand and a triumphant smile on her face.

"She must've got it for a major deal," said G-Baby from the front seat of his Escalade.

"My sis has a way with words that'll make a genius feel stupid."

G-Baby got out and hopped in the back seat so Yessy could ride shotgun with her baby bro.

"It's about time you smile, Yessy," Romeo said, looking at her.

She clicked her seatbelt on. "I'm hungry."

Romeo nodded. Glancing back at G-Baby, the Gangsta Boo shrugged. Romeo knew that Yessy was really upset. It'd been a week since she'd seen or heard from her man. Nobody, in fact, had heard from Macho, Tool, nor their grandparents.

YESSINIA

Leaning back, Yessy sighed once again after checking her missed call log, her texts, and even her email. Absolutely no word at all from her man. It was killing her. Tears welled up in her eyes. She had the worst feeling in her gut.

The growl of the 850-horsepower supercharged Hennessey Performance V8 under the Escalade's hood brought her back out of the deep recesses of her mind. She inhaled a deep breath, then exhaled, trying so hard to stay positive. Romeo put it in drive and pulled out of the parking spot. The Ford F-350 dually pickup truck with four Rastas toting choppers fell in behind him as he exited the parking lot and got onto Milwaukee Avenue, heading north.

G-Baby scooted up and down, reached out, and hugged Yessy. She leaned her head against the left side of Yessy's head and held her, reminding her that she wasn't alone.

Romeo reached over and took his sister's hand, holding it to assist G-Baby with the sentiment.

Yessy felt the love, no doubt. And because of the reason it was being displayed, it caused her to burst into tears.

G-Baby's own eyes welled up. The feelings she had for Macho—him being incognito and having seen news clips on her iPhone about the deadly shootout in the restaurant he'd told her he and his brother were going to, and the crazy shootout on the highway—had her emotions jumbled up.

"He'll be okay, sis," she said to Yessy, her voice breaking up as she spoke. "He's gonna be back for you really soon. I promise."

Romeo entered and passed through Gurnee. The Rastas were still right behind him. At the end of Milwaukee Ave, he came to a red light at Milwaukee and Route 41.

Yo Gotti's "LAW," featuring E-40, pounded from the woofers in the back. Yessy had managed to relax a little, thanks to G-Baby reminding her that her man was a straight gangster and had survived way worse situations than shootouts.

Yessy's iPhone screen lit up as it rested on her lap. She saw a text notification from ChaCha.

You trying to meet at Iron Skillet? ChaCha had asked.

Yessy texted back, telling her they were actually already en route, then gave her the news about inking a deal for the new property.

Congrats, mami! I'll meet y'all there. I have some news for you, ChaCha replied.

Reading those words immediately made Yessy sit up. She asked if it had anything to do with her man, Tool, and the ol' heads.

All I'll say is that they're all okay, but no, the news has to do with that car you've been looking for.

Sighing, Yessy knew what—and who—ChaCha was talking about. She sent a thumbs-up emoji, then set her iPhone back down on the center console.

ROMEO

The light turned green. Romeo made a left turn onto the highway and headed north, but seconds later came to another red light at 41 and Sterns School Road.

Nas's *Got Urself A…* was on. He nodded his head to the beat as he waited behind two other vehicles. Yessy was leaned back, her eyes closed. She'd stopped crying, which made him feel better.

In the back, G-Baby was chilling on her phone, playing a game. Looking back straight, Romeo's left peripheral caught movement in his mirror. It was a person, wearing a ski mask, creeping up alongside the Rastas' pickup truck with a duffel bag in hand. The guy then tossed it into the dooly's bed.

"Oh shit! Aye!" he shouted, panicking, keeping his horn blaring frantically.

Yessy's eyes shot open when she heard her brother. G-Baby immediately went for the AK-47 that was stashed in the gun rack under the floorboard at her feet.

They all looked back just as the four big Jamaicans hopped out with their AKs to blast the masked man.

Yessy quickly hit a spot on the dashboard and opened the hidden gun rack compartment, grabbing the altered fully automatic M4 Carbine, equipped with an extended magazine of 5.56 NATO rounds.

The Rastas were about to blow the masked man down, when suddenly...

BOOM!

The dually exploded from the C4 that the masked man tossed into the bed. The Rastas went flying. The car next to their pickup exploded before the people inside could get out.

Romeo gritted his teeth in pure anger as he saw a mob of other masked men running up on his SUV with assault rifles and shotguns. He reached down and grabbed the two 10-millimeter Tauruses his sister had altered and given to him.

The sound of tires screeching took his eyes off the rear and back out the windshield. A windowless van had skidded to a stop in the middle of the intersection, and hopping out were more masked men—with choppers and shotguns.

From the rear and from the front, the mob surrounded the Escalade. The people in the cars in front, beside, and behind the burning pickup and Ford Fusion screamed and attempted to get out of there.

"Go!" Yessy shouted when she saw one man who had jumped out of the van pull the pin on a grenade.

Romeo mashed the gas as the guy hurled it at the whip. The Caddy truck shot forward, ramming the vehicle in front of him, pushing it into the first car.

The shooters then opened fire, hitting innocent bystanders as they blew at the Escalade.

Bullets pinged off the SUV but didn't penetrate. The Escalade had been taken to an armoring business before it went to the Hennessey Performance factory down in Texas—then it became Yessy's bulletproof rocket.

The grenade exploded seconds after Romeo pushed his way out of the box. The gunmen dumped round after round as he flared it. They jumped back in their vehicles and gave chase, with no intentions of letting the loved ones of their boss's target get away.

G-BABY

"Roll the back window down!" she shouted, gripping the AK and pointing it at the rear window.

Yessy hit a button on the dash, dropping it down. Then she hit the button to roll the sunroof back.

G-Baby started dumping at the Dodge Charger SRT8 that led the others in pursuit. She sent rounds of 7.62s flying through the windshield, exploding the glass, while Yessy blew at the Scat Pack Durango behind it.

The Charger's two front occupants were hit. Their heads exploded. The SRT8 lost control and started skidding sideways, then caught a pothole. It started flipping repeatedly, going airborne and landing in the southbound lanes.

The shooters in the Durango fired back. Yessy dropped back down into the Escalade as bullets whizzed by her, millimeters from hitting her.

She hit the button for the back window, putting it back up before any shots could get inside.

Romeo kept his foot on the gas, hitting speeds of over 100 mph. A bend in the highway came up. He took it so fast he nearly flipped over.

The Durango, the van, and two other SUVs continued pursuing them, taking up both lanes and shooting at the Cadillac's rear end. The Scat Pack Durango and the SRT8 Jeep were the only ones fast enough to keep up with the Escalade, but none of them gave up the chase.

The interstate intersection for 41 and Wadsworth was coming up. Romeo cursed when he saw the light was red and vehicles were crossing through.

Yessy gasped, nervous about crashing. G-Baby braced herself.

"Hold on, yo!" Romeo shouted, gripping the wheel tightly.

Yessy held onto her seat and closed her eyes. Seconds later, she heard an explosion. Her eyes shot open. She turned to see the Durango had slammed into another vehicle, hitting it so hard they both flew into the BP gas station on the northbound side of the highway—hitting a gas pump and blazing up.

She cursed, happy they made it through the intersection unscathed but saddened by the fact that more people had just lost their lives—because of them.

The SRT8 Jeep, the van, and the Ford Expedition blew through the intersection, not slowing down at all.

On the right, Romeo sped past a D.O.T. truck weight station. Yessy muttered a curse when she saw it wasn't open.

Hijo de puta! she thought. Of all the times, now that fucking scale wants to be closed!

She remembered how the Illinois state troopers that operated the scale house were always there, pulling trucks in and going extra hard on violations—because they were bored.

"Aye! Yo, look," Romeo hollered, glancing in the mirror. Yessy and G-Baby looked back and saw two thick black plumes of smoke and fire shooting high up into the air behind the chasers.

"Yes! Yes! Yeeesss!" Yessy screamed excitedly, knowing exactly what was coming.

G-Baby's eyes filled with tears. Romeo took a second to figure it out, but when he heard the loud air horn blast, he knew.

"Macho! Yes! He's here!" Romeo shouted, relieved.

MACHO

He had the gas pedal to the floor, shifter all the way in 18th gear. All 1,400 horses roared, the dashboard reading 132 mph. Macho gritted his teeth and prepared for impact. Next to him, Tool held his 12-gauge, ready to handle business.

Behind them, El Viejo—the 5-star General—with the two ol' heads ready as well.

Macho got right up onto the Expedition's rear end and rammed it with enough force to send it flying over the concrete center divider into oncoming lanes.

He sped up, got on the van's bumper, slammed into it, and spun it. It fishtailed and started sliding. Without losing speed, he T-boned it, slicing through it like El Viejo was a hot steak knife and the van was butter.

The Scat Pack Durango started swerving, trying to evade him, as Romeo's Escalade reached the Route 41 and Route 173 intersection. Macho stayed on its tail, chasing it as it zigzagged through the intersection.

Two lanes of traffic waiting in the southbound lanes at the red light blocked the Durango's escape. The driver tried to whip it back to the right to jump onto I-73 and dip east—but Macho caught the rear passenger side of it.

El Viejo smacked the Durango off the road, sending it tumbling onto the grassy corner, landing on its roof. Macho slammed on the brakes, bringing his armored and heavy bobtail Peterbilt to a stop. He and his brother jumped out, not giving a damn about witnesses or the state police station just thirty seconds up the road. Juanito skidded his ol' school to a stop and jumped out with his wife to assist their grandsons.

YESSINIA

"Stop! Stop! Stooooop!" screamed Yessy, seeing her man and his people hop out of their ol' school rigs.

Romeo slammed the brakes and whipped the steering wheel left, spinning the Cadillac truck in a 180. He mashed the gas and shot back down south in the northbound lanes, speeding in the wrong direction.

G-Baby's eyes went to the right as they passed the weight station. A few tractor-trailers were parked inside, along with one Illinois State Police vehicle. She mentally urged everyone to hurry up and get out of there before swarms of state troopers and Lake County sheriffs came gunning for them all.

But before Romeo could get there, Yessy saw her man, his brother, and their grandfather muscling one of the shooters from the Durango into El Viejo. Carolina blasted the other two inside.

Tool had jumped up behind the wheel of the ol' school 359. His brother was back in the 63" box-shaped flat-top sleeper, and the ol' heads returned to the GMC General.

Yessy caught a glimpse of Tool pointing for them to follow, as he blew past them like a rocket engine was under El Viejo's hood.

"Turn around! Catch up!" Yessy urged her brother as Juanito flew his rig past them.

Romeo about-faced again and hit the gas, rocketing in the right direction now, hurrying to catch up with the two wickedly fast semi-trucks.

G-Baby looked to her left again as they came upon the weight station. She saw the state trooper outside, standing with a few truckers. It looked to her like the trooper had no intention of calling in reinforcements.

Knowing what she did about many Illinois State Police officers, the Valdez name was known and feared. She was sure that the reason the trooper wasn't radioing wasn't just because they were less than a minute away from crossing into Wisconsin—but because most sheriffs, agents, troopers, and other law enforcement officials did not want problems with the Valdez family.

Chapter 19

Yessy called Macho's phone as they crossed into Pleasant Prairie. She got excited when it actually rang. Four rings later, he answered.

"Numero Uno Transport, how may I assist you today?" he asked.

Yessy snapped. "¡Mamao! ¿Qué carajo? Why the hell has your phone been off?"

"I was in the cut, bae," Macho told her. "You know it was necessary to stay in the dark until the sun comes up, amor. Hold a second."

CRACK!

Yessy grimaced when she heard fist hitting face, then her man shouting:

"Shut up, bitch! Fuck is you cryin' for?"

CRACK! CRACK! CRACK!

"Take this ass whoopin' like a man, mamahuevo!"

CRACK!

"Okay. I'm back," she heard him say.

She burst out laughing as they flew past the shopping plaza with the big Nike Factory Outlet store.

"Anyway. Are y'all okay?" he asked.

"No! I swear to God I'm gonna kick your ass all over the place, Antonio!"

"Me too, asshole!" G-Baby shouted from the rear.

"Gabi said she's kickin' ya culo too," Yessy told him.

"Don't trip, bro! I got cha back!" Romeo hollered.

"Shut up, Romeo!" Yessy snapped.

"Hmmm…Romeo and me, against you and Gabi!" Macho said. "Brrrring it!" he challenged.

"Wrong, mamao! It's Gabi, me, ChaCha, Michelle, Eve—and probably all the others too!" she declared. "And if you run, I *will* catch you!"

"Grrrr! Love you!" he said, then ended the call.

Romeo reached over and patted his sister's shoulder.

G-Baby reached up and wrapped her arms around Yessy. "See? I told you he was gonna be okay, sis!"

Yessy nodded her head. "Yes, you did."

"And now you get to kick his ass while I beat the shit out of this bitchass mamabicho they snatched up," G-Baby added, already plotting how bad she was about to do the guy.

Up in Oak Creek, Wisconsin, Romeo followed the two rigs along a rocky dirt road until they arrived at a huge circular area with Lake Michigan next to it. They were surrounded by so many trees that he felt like they were somehow in the Amazon rainforest.

Almost, though. Parked there were three vehicles.

Posted in front of a cream soda colored 1988 AMG edition Mercedes Benz 560 Sl droptop sitting on gold BBS mesh wheels was the head of the Valdez family's Caribbean goon squad, Jamaica. He was a light skinned deadhead, standing 6-feet tall with an athletic figure, despite him being in his late 50s. His thick beard was spiced with grays as was his thick Rasta dreads. The man was dressed in just a black tank top, fatigue cargo pants, and black Timberland's on his feet. There was fire in his eyes from the news of what had happened to his men.

A very rare carbon fiber Koenigsegg CCXR was next to the Benz, and standing in front of it, was the big, bulky Xavier and the golden stallion Evelyn.

The third vehicle was so expensive that rich folks went broke trying to buy one. The silver and purple Pagani Zonda HP Borchetta was forever a convertible and came with Burberry plaid interior. In front of the beautiful Italian hyper car, her second one, was ChaCha, looking very much like a devilish diva in her sexy dress and heels while holding on AA12 shotgun, wearing a scowl on her face.

Yessy jumped out of the Caddy truck before Romeo could come to a complete stop and ran as fast as her 6-inch YSL pumps could carry her to her man, as he climbed down from the passenger's side of the ol' Pete, kicking the captured shooter out of the cab before him.

She ran right into his arms and wrapped her arms around him so tightly that he thought his ribs would crack.

"Don't you ever do this to me again, Antonio!" she screamed, tears pouring from her eyes as she buried her face in his chest.

Doing his best to control his own emotion, Macho leaned down and kissed the top of her head. He held her for a minute, letting her cry in his chest. Everyone stood silently for the two.

Almost everyone.

"Motherfucker!" someone yelled.

Looking back, Yessy and Macho saw the Gangsta Boo had pounced on the shooter like a hungry lioness. She was going apeshit on him, beating his face in with everything in her. His blood splattered her in the face every time she plopped him. Tool ran over to her, pulling her up off of the guy before she killed him.

"Sueltae, Tool! Let me gooooo!"

"Naw, Gabi. Me and bro got a few questions for this clown," Tool told her, carrying her over to where the Valdez family's version of Jennifer Lopez/Griselda Blanco stood.

"Tranquila, nena," ChaCha said to her, waiting for the wild card to do what she did best.

Jamica walked up to Macho, his woman, and now Tool stood. Juanito and Carolina walked up to them a second later. They all looked at the bloody man laying on the ground, writhing in pain.

"Make de bombaclot muddafucka feel de worst pain for what him did to me buddaz, ya 'ear me, Tiguere?" Jamaica said to Macho.

He smirked and nodded. "Nothin' less, tio," he replied, then Macho lifted his woman's face to make her look at him. "I'll be right back, amor. Voy a ensenarle, a ese mamahuevo lo que le pasa a la gente cuando Joden commigo puneta."

Kissing her lips, she put a smile on her face.

He smiled back, then looked at his brother. "Hop up in El Viejo, 'mano," Macho told Tool. "This nigga gon' learn today, yo. Homiez!"

G-BABY

She gasped in shock when she saw him actually climb up on the roof of the old Peterbilt, pulling the injured shooter with him. Romeo was amazed. Yessy was wowed by his strength. Carolina, now standing with ChaCha, Evelyn, Xavier, Jamaica, and her husband, smirked as she watched her crazy grandson work.

Behind the wheel, Tool had the powerful CAT engine on and idling, waiting for his brother to give word.

G-Baby saw the shooter struggling to get free of Macho's strong grip.

Macho laughed, holding the guy up in the air. G-Baby heard him demand the guy to tell them who he was sent by. The guy defiantly told him, "Tu madre, puto!"

"Oooo...he just fucked up," G-Baby said to herself, knowing how sensitive the topic of Macho and Tool's deceased mother was.

Hell. It made her even angrier to hear the guy say, "Your mother, bitch!"

She then saw Macho turn into the demon she knew all too well that he could be.

"Bro! Hit the gas!" she heard Macho holler to his brother.

While he lifted the man up high enough, putting his face right above the tip of the driver's side 7-inch diameter exhaust stack, Tool hit the gas pedal, revving the engine.

Everyone watched as fire shot out of both of the stacks. The shooter screamed in agony as his face was severely burned by the fiery flames.

"Yeeeeaaah, bitch! Baptism by fire! God fuck you!" Macho yelled as he continued hold the man to the flames.

"Hooooly shhit!" G-Baby gasped, flabbergasted and turned on.

They all then heard the shooter scream, "Okay! Okay!" now ready to talk.

Macho tossed him off of the truck. He hit the ground hard. Tool let off of the gas and hopped out with a machete in his hand. G-Baby and Romeo hurried over to where Yessy stood with her fists balled, ready to see the guy die.

YESSINIA

"El demonio! It was el demonio that hired us!" The guy ratted. "he told us you killed pancho?"

She saw her man glance at her, shake his head, then looked back at the burned shooter.

"My man…El Demonio is dead. Trust me, try again."

"No! No, he's not! My people just talked to him, man!"

Macho's eyebrows furrowed. He looked at the guy in his eyes.

"I know he's Tejano, and he's a Latin King, bro! He's not dead!"

Yessy's eyebrows furrowed. She glanced over at G-Baby who looked like she was thinking the same thing.

"A King, huh? I heard he was a MP," Macho said to the guy.

"No! He is a King! I swear!"

Just then, Tool called to Yessy. She went over to him. He handed her the machete.

"Check it. This is what's gonna happen, mamahuevo," Macho told the guy. "You are going to say you're sorry to my lady and…Gabi! Rome! Ven!" he hollered to the other two that could've been killed as well. They hurried over to him and stood with Yessy. "My homegirl and my lil man's," Macho continued. "If they are not satisfied, and feel your apology is not truly heartfelt...my lady will literally split your wig."

"I'm s—"

WHACK!

Yessy didn't even let him finish. She raised the machete up high over her head and brought it down as hard as she could. The blade sliced right through his face, splitting it vertically, silencing him forever.

"Okay...you could've at least let him say sorry, bae," Macho said as she yanked the machete out of the man's face.

Four Chevy Suburbans entered the lot right then and out came sixteen dread-heads— two of them with flame throwers.

"I'm hungry," Yessy told her man, then walked off towards El Viejo.

Macho chuckled. "I'm famished, too. Iron Skillet anybody?"

"We were already, headin there," G-Baby told him.

"Me hungry, too," Jamaica added, then told his two goons to take care of the dead shooter.

The dreads put fire to the corpse and roasted it until there was ashes. The family all got back into their vehicles and rolled out to make their way to their favorite truck stop restaurant.

MACHO

Macho exited 94 in Sturtevant and headed to the popular restaurant that sat right along the interstate and highway 20. Juanito and Carolina were behind him and his woman. The others went to the noncommercial parking area in front of the Iron Skillet, while Macho and Juanito parked in the truck lot in between the restaurant and a Petro Lube truck repair shop. The ol' heads hopped out of the General and headed towards the restaurant.

Macho cut the engine off and was about to get out when Yessy stopped him.

"Where do you think you are going, Mister?" she asked, getting up from her seat.

"Um." Macho looked at her. "You said you was hungry."

"Oh, I am starving, but right now, I'm hungry for you," she told him, then she grabbed his shirt and forced him back into the luxurious sleeper berth.

Macho laughed as she started ridding him of his clothes. In less than fifteen seconds, she had him all the way undressed. Yessy bit her lip as she took a second to look at him. His muscular frame, tattooed python size arms, toned thighs, runners legs. He loved to eat, so, although he didn't have a six pack, his stomach was still sort of flat.

On his left pectoral muscle, he had *STEEL CITY MAFIA* with a picture-perfect image of his prized Legacy Class Edition Peterbilt 379 Extended Hood under it. In the grille of the tatted semi, his mother's name, and his father's under it. Her favorite flower was a rose, and her favorite color was blue.

Yessy's eyes fell down to his bone-hard cock. His erection pointed right at her, pulsating before her very eyes. Her mouth watered at the sight of it.

"Uh oh," Macho said, knowing that look way too well.

Yessy went and dropped to her knees before him, wasting no time taking his dick into her mouth. She stuffed him back into her throat and went nuts on him.

"Fuck!" Macho cursed from her phenomenal skills.

Yessy spit his dick out, licked and sucked on his balls, then took him back into her mouth. With two hands she jerked and sucked, looking like she was playing a flute.

"Goddammit! Cono, Mamita!" Macho groaned as his head spun in circles.

Macho took his dick away from her and yanked her up off the floor. He made her assume the position. Grabbing the bed, Yessy bent over. She grew even hotter as Macho undid her leather belt and dropped her skin-tight Saint Laurent jeans down. He pulled her thong out of her ass crack and slid into her wetness from behind. Immediately, he started jackhammering her, making Yessy scream out in bliss. He hit it hard and fast, smacking her ass, pulling her hair. She exploded on his dick minutes later, coating him in her juices.

He pulled out and leaned down, burying his face between her juicy cheeks. Yessy squealed as he licked up and down her crack, swirling his tongue around her butthole. She shrieked when she felt him stick his tongue inside it.

"Shit, Antonio! Oh my God, I fucking love you!"

He snaked his tongue around inside her chute then ejected it. He spit on her asshole then uprighted himself. He smacked her cheek. "You ready for me, baby?" he asked her.

"Yes! Fuck me, papi!" Yessy pleaded as she rested her face on the bed, reaching back and opening her ass up for him. "Damelo el bicho, pape! Ahora mismo!"

Macho eased his wet cock into Yessy's asshole, careful not to hurt her. As he slow-stroked her, she got acclimated to him, begging him to give it to her.

He went harder on her for almost ten minutes before she climaxed again. He felt his nut coming soon after. Yessy felt his dick spasming inside of her and reached back to pull him out so she could give him a grand finale nut.

Back on her knees, she opened her mouth wide. Macho put it back in her mouth and groaned as Yessy sucked him until he busted his nut in her mouth. With one hand, she jerked him while she milked him. When he was empty, and her mouth was full, she spat it all out on his dick, then lapped his cum back up and swallowed.

"Holy smiggadiesmoke!" Macho said, pulling her up from the floor. "You are a freak!"

Yessy smiled. "I'm just happy you're back with me, Antonio. I'm for real; don't leave me like that again."

"I won't, my love. My word I won't."

"Good, because if you do, I'm going to bite you in your sleep, and I'm going to bite somewhere it will really hurt."

"Violent ass porkchop."

"Mmmm…porkchops." Yessy's stomach growled. "Time to go eat. Let's go!"

Inside the restaurant, Macho held his woman's hand as they were led to where everyone was seated in rear section. Tables were put together to accommodate the nine of them. Macho pulled out a chair for his woman and sat her down, pushing her up to the table. He sat next to her, then a waiter came to take their drink and food orders.

"I gotta make a call real quick, bae," he said to her then, remembering what the Ecuadorian had said. He felt eyes on him as he got back up and left, but he didn't care. He was boiling inside. Macho exited the restaurant and called Narco.

"What up, my nigga?" Narco answered on the third ring.

"Yo, why is it a little birdie swears up and down that the guy we went to go have a chat with was not who you told me he was?"

"Hold up...what?"

"Nigga, you heard what I said, yo. This is not the time to play deaf."

"Bro, I do not know what the fuck you talkin' about. But if it wasn't him, don't chu think yo shit would still be leavin' muhfuckas laid out?" Narco said. "Cause I ain't been hearin' that. Shit dun' got replaced from what it sounds like. Money's back flowin'. Who the hell is this birdie?"

"One that can't fly no more."

"Well, fuck him. And fuck all that other shit. Is you and yo' bro cool?" asked Narco.

"Why wouldn't we be?"

"Maaan, come on, dog, you know I heard what happened. I can't make sure my boy is safe?"

"You're talking to me. That should say it all."

"Well, where you at now, bro? I'll come slide on you and we can have a drink or something. I was worried about y'all niggas, dog."

"Rain check. I'm with family. Holla," Macho said, then he ended the call. For a few minutes, he stood there. He had a bad feeling that he couldn't shake. Something wasn't right. He felt it in his bones. Making his way back inside, he brushed it all off…for now, so he could enjoy some time with his woman and his family.

YESSINIA

"What about Yayo?" asked Yessy, referring to ChaCha's newest addition to her stable of killers.

"Oh, he is definitely ready to start handlin' business, Momita," ChaCha informed her. "And for how things are looking…all my babies are gonna be having a lot of work to do."

"Any word on that Vito nigga yet?" G-Baby asked as Macho rejoined them.

"He's in the wind, ma," said ChaCha, watching him sit next to Yessy.

"Him will be caught, though, Gorilla Mama," Jamaica assured her. "Me got eyes searching for de pussyhole muddfucka. Soon him will be caught."

"Until then," ChaCha spoke again, looking at Macho, Yessy and G-Baby, "you all need to go somewhere and kick back. We will start cleaning up."

"But we can—"

"No! I said go." ChaCha cut Macho off, putting her foot down on the matter. "Go to Pittsburgh or the D.R. Just go for a while, yo."

Yessy started grinning at the idea of a getaway. G-Baby did, too.

Seeing the smiles on their faces, Macho agreed. "Okay. We'll take a little vacation," he said, "but we ain't goin' to the 'Purgh, nor the D.R."

"Then…where?" his grandmother asked with the same puzzled expression on her face that everyone else had.

Macho cheesed up. "We goin' to…White People World! Dah dah dah daaah!"

Yessy and G-Baby exchanged glances with each other. They were both extremely confused now. The only person that knew where Macho was talking about was Tool. He busted out laughing at his brother. The family looked at the Steel City mafia goons, waiting for an explanation.

"Care to elaborate, Antonio?" ChaCha asked.

"Nope. But while y'all get it on 'n poppin', we gon' have a little fun in the sun. Are y'all ready?"

Yessy and G-Baby both frowned at him.

He smiled broadly. "Good!"

***

Back at their home, Macho pulled El Viejo up to the front door and parked. Behind him followed Romeo, ChaCha and Tool. The ol' heads parted ways after dining on delicious meals, along with Xavier, Evelyn, and the Rastas.

Macho put Tool in charge of Numero Uno until he and the ladies returned. Romeo was happy to be given a little say-so by Yessy. She and G-Baby scheduled him on their D.O.D contract, instructing him on things he'd be hauling to and from, and with whom. He was glad to hear that a lot of his runs would be with DBoy, whom Yessy put in charge of the heavy vehicle/machinery transportation of the contracted work.

With a concrete plan agreed upon, Romeo and Tool were good to go. ChaCha was included to help out, which was all good with her. It'd give her another reason to be out of the office and behind the wheel of her extensively decked out X Edition Peterbilt.

***

Just over an hour later, Macho, Yessy and G-Baby were packed up and ready to go where Macho still hadn't revealed.

"Baaee!" Yessy whined, wrapping her arms around him from behind as he tossed XL goldfish to his caimans, watching them snap the goldfish up like it'd been days since they'd eaten. "Where are we going?"

"To White People World!" he announced like a deep-voiced TV show host.

"Come on, man! For real!"

Macho threw the last fish and watched Dino catch it. He turned around and put his arms around his lady's body, hugging her to him. "Okay. I'll tell you, but don't tell Gabbi."

Yessy smiled and nodded.

"We are going...tooo…White People World!"

Her smile vanished and her eyes narrowed. She called him an asshole and walked off to go find G-Baby.

"It's okay! It's ookay!" He hollered, imitating Scarface. "When we get 'der…she be happy!"

Yessy and G-Baby stood outside of another one of their houses, waiting for Macho to pull out of the two-car garage. He backed out a new Extreme Silver-Colored Bently Mulsanne LeMans edition, and came to stop in front of them.

G-Baby looked at the big Bentley, nodding in approval. Its paint flicked so hard, even as daylight faded. The 23-inch chrome Forgiatos had B-center caps, and Forgiato engraved on the rims' wide lips. Chrome trim, custom grille, wood grain and chrome inside the exclusive seashell-colored leather interior. It made her want to go drop $440,000 on a LeMans Mulsanne of her own.

Macho put the bags in the trunk as Yessy and G-Baby got in the car. As he hit a button electronically closing the trunk, he pulled his iPhone and backed out of the driveway, exiting out the gate, and turning left onto Green Bay Road he headed north.

Yessy reached over to the LCD screen and put on some music. When Mike Jones's *Cuddybuddy* featuring Trey Songz, T-Pain, Twista, and Lil Wayne started bumping from the stock Burmester audio system, she reached over and took her man's hand and held onto it, never wanting to let it go.

Chapter 20

G-BABY

She opened her eyes after yet another dream. The kind that left her with wet panties from such real visions, of him and her, naked on a beach in Negril, going strong and long, pleasing each other right in front of other people.

As her vision cleared up, she saw the gargantuan building on the right with a big water slide jutting out of it, wrapping around the corner and reentering the building. On the main side of the building, G-Baby saw Kalahari. Immediately, she knew where they were going. It made her laugh to herself. At least she thought it was to herself.

The music lowered. Macho spoke as he got into the exit lane to get off of 94. "Y'all must've stayed up the whole five days all the crazy shit was poppin' off," he told her.

G-Baby realized that Yessy was K.O.'d in the front seat.

"It's kind of hard to sleep when you're worried about someone you love," she said, then instantly regretted it.

"Aw, lemme find out the Gangsta Boo loves me, yo," Macho teased as he exited the highway.

She got real quiet. Her face got hot. She started blushing.

"I was just playin', Gabi." Macho chuckled.

"Hush, punk ass," she replied, then sat back as Macho made a right turn onto the main road that ran right through Wisconsin Dells.

It'd been a few years since she had been to Dells. Seeing the hotels, motels, restaurants, and the big water park on her right made G-Baby smile. Further along, Macho passed

Treasure Island, an indoor water park-resort that was almost as big as the Kalahari. Next to it was Mount Olympus, a big section with multiple go-kart tracks, a few rollercoasters, a concession spot, a water ride, and a big arcade. It was most known for the gigantic, sky-high wooden Trojan Horse that go-kart races raced through, going up on one side and then sped down the other side.

Across from Mount Olympus was a building where vacationers could feed alligators. Another building offered a go-kart track, and beyond its parking lot, a boarding stand for those that desired a tour ride on one of the famous Dells Duck ampfibus.

Macho passed both roadside spots. G-Baby sighed, realizing that they weren't going to Treasure Island like they normally went to.

He started ascending a huge hill then. Cresting the top, he rolled through a small 3-way intersection, passing more roadside attractions. Another big go-kart park with a waterpark was across from a house that was completely upside down, and next to it, a small shack that a man posted in, ready to give thrill rides in the helicopter he combined with a monster truck out on the dirt track through the woods behind his shack.

He descended another massive hill. Merging down into the left turn lane, G-Baby saw the other exclusive hotel built to replicate a luxurious city of log cabins, situated on a snow-covered mountain out in Aspen, Colorado.

After Macho hit a left at the light at the bottom of the hill, he got in the right lane, killing G-Baby's hopes of going to the log cabin hotel.

He rolled past Paul Bunyan's Wisconsin Dells famous and very popular eatery, which served the best breakfast a human with tastebuds could get.

Yessy moaned as she began to stir. G-Baby sat in her seat, putting her arms around the Nuyorican.

"Ooo! The Dells!" Yessy realized as Macho slowed down with his right turn signal on, to make the turn into the parking lot of a hotel called The Polynesian. Yessy busted out laughing when she realized that he was calling Wisconsin Dells *White People World*. "Bae, you're funny as hell. It's not just white people that come here."

Macho laughed. "Damn near," he replied, finding a parking spot across from the 2-story hotel building.

G-Baby chuckled, shaking her head at him.

MACHO

He backed the Mulsanne in between two other cars. A few people walking past broke their necks to get a good look at the fine automobile, and to see who was in it.

Getting out, Macho opened the trunk and grabbed their luggage. He closed it back, then with Yessy and G-Baby behind him, Macho led them in the direction of the hotel's entrance.

Right as he stepped into the middle of the passing lane, a blood red Rolls Royce Phantom on big red rims sped up to him and skidded sideways to a stop.

Yessy and G-Baby jumped as Macho dropped the luggage and stood in front of them, ready to have taken the hit for them.

The driver's door opened up a second later and out hopped a large man in all black with a goblin mask on, and two pistols in his hands, pointing them right at Macho with his fingers wrapped around their triggers.

He laughed hysterically at the shocked looks on their faces, then he shouted, "Yeah, nigga! Got cho' ass now, foo!" right before he let them both go...

To Be Continued...

Lock Down Publications and Ca$h Presents Assisted Publishing Packages

Due to an increase in the price of services we have increased our prices. The prices below reflect the price increase as of 11/1/24.

BASIC PACKAGE **$699** Editing Cover Design Formatting	**UPGRADED PACKAGE** **$1000** Typing Editing Cover Design Formatting Upload eBooks to Amazon Upload Paperback to Amazon
ADVANCE PACKAGE **$1,400** Typing Editing (line editing/content) Cover Design Formatting Copyright Registration Proofreading Upload eBooks to Amazon Upload Paperback to Amazon	**LDP SUPREME PACKAGE** **$1,700** Typing Editing (line editing/content) Cover Design Formatting Copyright Registration Proofreading Set up Amazon Account Upload eBooks to Amazon Upload Paperback to Amazon Advertise on LDP's Amazon and Facebook Page

***

Other services available upon request.
Additional charges may apply

Lock Down Publications
P.O. Box 944
Stockbridge, GA 30281-9998
Phone: 470 303-9761
Email: lockdownpublications@gmail.com

Submission Guideline

Submit the first three chapters of your completed manuscript to ldpsubmissions@gmail.com. In the subject line add **Your Book's Title**. The manuscript must be in a Word Doc file and sent as an attachment. Document should be in Times New Roman, double spaced, and in size 12 font. Also, provide your synopsis and full contact information. If sending multiple submissions, they must each be in a separate email.

Have a story but no way to send it electronically? You can still submit to LDP/Ca$h Presents. Send in the first three chapters, written or typed, of your completed manuscript to:

LDP: Submissions Dept
P.O. Box 944
Stockbridge, GA 30281-9998

DO NOT send original manuscript. Must be a duplicate. Provide your synopsis and a cover letter containing your full contact information.

Thanks for considering LDP and Ca$h Presents.

NEW RELEASES

BLOODLINE OF A SAVAGE 1-3
THESE VICIOUS STREETS 1-3
RELENTLESS GOON 1-3
BY PRINCE A. TAUHID

THE BUTTERFLY MAFIA 1-3
BY FUMIYA PAYNE

A THUG'S STREET PRINCESS 1&2
BY MEESHA

CITY OF SMOKE 3
BY MOLOTTI

GET IT IN SLUGS 1 &2
BY B. STALL

STANDING ON HER BUSINESS 1&2
BY DG SANTANA

STEPPERS 1,2&3
THE REAL BADDIES OF CHI-RAQ
BY KING RIO

THE LANE 1&2
BY KEN-KEN SPENCE

THUG OF SPADES 1&2
LOVE IN THE TRENCHES 2
CORNER BOYS
BY COREY ROBINSON

TIL DEATH 3
BY ARYANNA

THE BIRTH OF A GANGSTER 4
BY DELMONT PLAYER

PRODUCT OF THE STREETS 1-3
BY DEMOND "MONEY" ANDERSON

NO TIME FOR ERROR
BY KEESE

MONEY HUNGRY DEMONS 1-2
BY TRANAY ADAMS

HUB CITY MENACE 1-3
BY J. WHITE

A THUGGISH PASSION 1&2
LAND OF DA HOOLIGANZ 1-4
KILLAZ ON STANDBY 1&2
BY IRA B.

FO'EVA ROLLIN 1&2
BY ASSA RAYMOND BAKER

THE LEVEL UP 1&3
BY LUXURY KING

Coming Soon from Lock Down Publications/Ca$h Presents

IF YOU CROSS ME ONCE 6
ANGEL V
By Anthony Fields

A THUGS STREET PRINCESS 3
By Meesha

CORNER BOYS 2
By Corey Robinson

THA TAKEOVER
By Keith Chandler

BETRAYAL OF A G 2
By Ray Vinci

SAVAGE FAMILY EMPIRE 1&2
SOULLESS GOON 1,2&3
THE DIRTY SIDE OF MONEY 1,2&3
By Prince

FOR MY ENEMY'S SAKE
AMBITIONS OF A SLIDER
FRESH OFF DA PORCH
By IRA B.

THE TRUCKLOAD 1-4
TIPPIN' THE SCALES 1-3
BAD BITCHES WIT GUNZ 3
PROBLEM SOLVED 2
By Christopher "Diesel" Hornezes

Available Now

RESTRAINING ORDER 1 & 2
By **CA$H & Coffee**

LOVE KNOWS NO BOUNDARIES 1-3
By **Coffee**

RAISED AS A GOON I, II, III & IV
BRED BY THE SLUMS I, II, III
BLAST FOR ME I & II
ROTTEN TO THE CORE I II III
A BRONX TALE I, II, III
DUFFLE BAG CARTEL I II III IV V VI
HEARTLESS GOON I II III IV V
A SAVAGE DOPEBOY I II
DRUG LORDS I II III
CUTTHROAT MAFIA I II
KING OF THE TRENCHES
By **Ghost**

LAY IT DOWN I & II
LAST OF A DYING BREED I II
BLOOD STAINS OF A SHOTTA I & II III
By **Jamaica**

LOYAL TO THE GAME I II III
LIFE OF SIN I, II III
By **TJ & Jelissa**

IF LOVING HIM IS WRONG…I & II
LOVE ME EVEN WHEN IT HURTS I II III
By **Jelissa**

PUSH IT TO THE LIMIT
By **Bre' Hayes**

BLOODY COMMAS I & II
SKI MASK CARTEL I, II & III
KING OF NEW YORK I II, III IV V
RISE TO POWER I II III
COKE KINGS I II III IV V
BORN HEARTLESS I II III IV
KING OF THE TRAP I II
By **T.J. Edwards**

WHEN THE STREETS CLAP BACK I & II III
THE HEART OF A SAVAGE I II III IV
MONEY MAFIA I II
LOYAL TO THE SOIL I II III
By **Jibril Williams**

A DISTINGUISHED THUG STOLE MY HEART I II & III
LOVE SHOULDN'T HURT I II III IV
RENEGADE BOYS 1-4
PAID IN KARMA 1-3
SAVAGE STORMS 1-3
AN UNFORESEEN LOVE 1-3
BABY, I'M WINTERTIME COLD 1-3
A THUG'S STREET PRINCESS 1&2
By **Meesha**

A GANGSTER'S CODE 1-3
A GANGSTER'S SYN 1-3
THE SAVAGE LIFE 1-3
CHAINED TO THE STREETS 1-3
BLOOD ON THE MONEY 1-3
A GANGSTA'S PAIN 1-3
BEAUTIFUL LIES AND UGLY TRUTHS
CHURCH IN THESE STREETS
By **J-Blunt**

CUM FOR ME 1-8
An LDP Erotica Collaboration

BLOOD OF A BOSS 1-5
SHADOWS OF THE GAME
TRAP BASTARD
By **Askari**

THE STREETS BLEED MURDER 1-3
THE HEART OF A GANGSTA 1-3
By **Jerry Jackson**

WHEN A GOOD GIRL GOES BAD
By **Adrienne**

THE COST OF LOYALTY 1-3
By **Kweli**

BRIDE OF A HUSTLA 1-3
THE FETTI GIRLS 1-3
CORRUPTED BY A GANGSTA 1-4
BLINDED BY HIS LOVE
THE PRICE YOU PAY FOR LOVE 1-3
DOPE GIRL MAGIC 1-3
By **Destiny Skai**

A KINGPIN'S AMBITION
A KINGPIN'S AMBITION II
I MURDER FOR THE DOUGH
By **Ambitious**

TRUE SAVAGE 1-7
DOPE BOY MAGIC 1-3
MIDNIGHT CARTEL 1-3
CITY OF KINGZ 1&2
NIGHTMARE ON SILENT AVE
THE PLUG OF LIL MEXICO 1&2
CLASSIC CITY
By **Chris Green**

A GANGSTER'S REVENGE 1-4
THE BOSS MAN'S DAUGHTERS 1-5
A SAVAGE LOVE 1&2
BAE BELONGS TO ME 1&2
A HUSTLER'S DECEIT 1-3
WHAT BAD BITCHES DO 1-3
SOUL OF A MONSTER 1-3
KILL ZONE
A DOPE BOY'S QUEEN 1-3
TIL DEATH 1-3
IMMA DIE BOUT MINE 1-6
DYING FOR LIKES
By **Aryanna**

A DOPEBOY'S PRAYER
By **Eddie "Wolf" Lee**

THE KING CARTEL 1-3
By **Frank Gresham**

THESE NIGGAS AIN'T LOYAL 1-3
By **Nikki Tee**

GANGSTA SHYT 1-3
By **CATO**

THE ULTIMATE BETRAYAL
By **Phoenix**

BOSS'N UP 1-3
By **Royal Nicole**

I LOVE YOU TO DEATH
By **Destiny J**

I RIDE FOR MY HITTA
I STILL RIDE FOR MY HITTA
By **Misty Holt**

LOVE & CHASIN' PAPER
By **Qay Crockett**

TO DIE IN VAIN
SINS OF A HUSTLA
By **ASAD**

BROOKLYN HUSTLAZ
By **Boogsy Morina**

BROOKLYN ON LOCK 1 & 2
By **Sonovia**

GANGSTA CITY
By **Teddy Duke**

A DRUG KING AND HIS DIAMOND 1-3
A DOPEMAN'S RICHES
HER MAN, MINE'S TOO 1&2
CASH MONEY HO'S
THE WIFEY I USED TO BE 1&2
PRETTY GIRLS DO NASTY THINGS
By **Nicole Goosby**

LIPSTICK KILLAH 1-3
CRIME OF PASSION 1-3
FRIEND OR FOE 1-3
By **Mimi**

TRAPHOUSE KING 1-3
KINGPIN KILLAZ 1-3
STREET KINGS 1&2
PAID IN BLOOD 1&2
CARTEL KILLAZ 1-3
DOPE GODS 1&2
By **Hood Rich**

THE STREETS ARE CALLING
By **Duquie Wilson**

STEADY MOBBN' 1-3
THE STREETS STAINED MY SOUL 1-3
By **Marcellus Allen**

WHO SHOT YA 1-3
SON OF A DOPE FIEND 1-4
HEAVEN GOT A GHETTO 1&2
SKI MASK MONEY 1&2
By **Renta**

GORILLAZ IN THE BAY 1-4
TEARS OF A GANGSTA 1/&2
3X KRAZY 1&2
STRAIGHT BEAST MODE 1&2
By **DE'KARI**

TRIGGADALE 1-3
MURDA WAS THE CASE 1-3
By **Elijah R. Freeman**

SLAUGHTER GANG 1-3
RUTHLESS HEART 1-3
By **Willie Slaughter**

GOD BLESS THE TRAPPERS 1-3
THESE SCANDALOUS STREETS 1-3
FEAR MY GANGSTA 1-5
THESE STREETS DON'T LOVE NOBODY 1-2
BURY ME A G 1-5
A GANGSTA'S EMPIRE 1-4
THE DOPEMAN'S BODYGAURD 1&2
THE REALEST KILLAZ 1-3
THE LAST OF THE OGS 1-3
By **Tranay Adams**

MARRIED TO A BOSS 1-3
By **Destiny Skai & Chris Green**

KINGZ OF THE GAME 1-7
CRIME BOSS 1-4
By **Playa Ray**

FUK SHYT
By **Blakk Diamond**

DON'T F#CK WITH MY HEART 1&2
By **Linnea**

ADDICTED TO THE DRAMA 1-3
IN THE ARM OF HIS BOSS
By **Jamila**

LOYALTY AIN'T PROMISED 1&2
By **Keith Williams**

YAYO 1-4
A SHOOTER'S AMBITION 1&2
BRED IN THE GAME
By **S. Allen**

TRAP GOD 1-3
RICH $AVAGE 1-3
MONEY IN THE GRAVE 1-3
CARTEL MONEY 1&2
By **Martell Troublesome Bolden**

FOREVER GANGSTA 1&2
GLOCKS ON SATIN SHEETS 1&2
By **Adrian Dulan**

TOE TAGZ 1-4
LEVELS TO THIS SHYT 1&2
IT'S JUST ME AND YOU
By **Ah'Million**

KINGPIN DREAMS 1-3
RAN OFF ON DA PLUG
By **Paper Boi Rari**

THE STREETS MADE ME 1-3
By **Larry D. Wright**

CONFESSIONS OF A GANGSTA 1-4
CONFESSIONS OF A JACKBOY 1-3
CONFESSIONS OF A HITMAN
CONFESSIONS OF A DOPE BOY
By **Nicholas Lock**

I'M NOTHING WITHOUT HIS LOVE
SINS OF A THUG
TO THE THUG I LOVED BEFORE
A GANGSTA SAVED XMAS
IN A HUSTLER I TRUST
By **Monet Dragun**

QUIET MONEY 1-3
THUG LIFE 1-3
EXTENDED CLIP 1&2
A GANGSTA'S PARADISE
By **Trai'Quan**

CAUGHT UP IN THE LIFE 1-3
THE STREETS NEVER LET GO 1-3
By **Robert Baptiste**

NEW TO THE GAME 1-3
MONEY, MURDER & MEMORIES 1-3
By **Malik D. Rice**

CREAM 2-3
THE STREETS WILL TALK
By **Yolanda Moore**

THE STREETS WILL NEVER CLOSE 1-3
By **K'ajji**

LIFE OF A SAVAGE 1-4
A GANGSTA'S QUR'AN 1-4
MURDA SEASON 1-3
GANGLAND CARTEL 1-3
CHI'RAQ GANGSTAS 1-4
KILLERS ON ELM STREET 1-3
JACK BOYZ N DA BRONX 1-3
A DOPEBOY'S DREAM 1-3
JACK BOYS VS DOPE BOYS 1-3
COKE GIRLZ
COKE BOYS
SOSA GANG 1&2
BRONX SAVAGES
BODYMORE KINGPINS
BLOOD OF A GOON
By **Romell Tukes**

CONCRETE KILLA 1-3
VICIOUS LOYALTY 1-3
BLOODY MONEY BAGS
By **Kingpen**

THE ULTIMATE SACRIFICE 1-6
KHADIFI
IF YOU CROSS ME ONCE 1-3
ANGEL 1-4
IN THE BLINK OF AN EYE
By **Anthony Fields**

THE LIFE OF A HOOD STAR
By **Ca$h & Rashia Wilson**

NIGHTMARES OF A HUSTLA 1-3
BLOOD AND GAMES 1&2
By **King Dream**

GHOST MOB
By **Stilloan Robinson**

HARD AND RUTHLESS 1&2
MOB TOWN 251
THE BILLIONAIRE BENTLEYS 1-3
REAL G'S MOVE IN SILENCE
By **Von Diesel**

MOB TIES 1-7
SOUL OF A HUSTLER, HEART OF A KILLER 1-3
GORILLAZ IN THE TRENCHES
OOPS CRY TOO 1&2
THE DAUGHTER OF A CARTEL BOSS
By **SayNoMore**

BODYMORE MURDERLAND 1-3
THE BIRTH OF A GANGSTER 1-4
By **Delmont Player**

FOR THE LOVE OF A BOSS 1&2
By **C. D. Blue**

KILLA KOUNTY 1-5
TENDER
By **Khufu**

MOBBED UP 1-4
THE BRICK MAN 1-5
THE COCAINE PRINCESS 1-10
STEPPERS 1-3
SUPER GREMLIN 1-4
A GANGSTA'S SON
By **King Rio**

MONEY GAME 1&2
By **Smoove Dolla**

A GANGSTA'S KARMA 1-5
By **FLAME**

KING OF THE TRENCHES 1-3
By **GHOST & TRANAY ADAMS**

BAD BITCHES WIT GUNZ 1&2
PROBLEM SOLVED
By "Christopher Diesel" Hornezes

QUEEN OF THE ZOO 1&2
By **Black Migo**

GRIMEY WAYS 1-3
BETRAYAL OF A G
By **Ray Vinci**

XMAS WITH AN ATL SHOOTER
By **Ca$h & Destiny Skai**

KING KILLA 1&2
By **Vincent "Vitto" Holloway**

BETRAYAL OF A THUG 1&2
By **Fre$h**

COUNTDOWN OF A KILLA 1&2
SEX, MURDER AND GOD 1&2
GUNS DOWN, BOTTOMS UP 1&2
By Lo-Life

THE MURDER QUEENS 1-7
By **Michael Gallon**

FOR THE LOVE OF BLOOD 1-4
By **Jamel Mitchell**

HOOD CONSIGLIERE 1&2
NO TIME FOR ERROR
By **Keese**

PROTÉGÉ OF A LEGEND 1,2&3
LOVE IN THE TRENCHES 1&2
By **Corey Robinson**

THE PLUG'S RUTHLESS DAUGHTER 1&2
By **Tony Daniels**

BORN IN THE GRAVE 1-3
CRIME PAYS
By **Self Made Tay**

MOAN IN MY MOUTH
By **XTASY**

TORN BETWEEN A GANGSTER AND A GENTLEMAN
By **J-BLUNT & Miss Kim**

LOYALTY IS EVERYTHING 1-3
CITY OF SMOKE 1-3
By **Molotti**

HERE TODAY GONE TOMORROW 1&2
By **Fly Rock**

WOMEN LIE MEN LIE 1-4
FIFTY SHADES OF SNOW 1-3
STACK BEFORE YOU SPLURGE
GIRLS FALL LIKE DOMINOES
NAÏVE TO THE STREETS
By **ROY MILLIGAN**

PILLOW PRINCESS
By **S. Hawkins**

THE BUTTERFLY MAFIA 1-3
SALUTE MY SAVAGERY 1&2
By **Fumiya Payne**

THE LANE 1&2
By Ken-Ken Spence

THE PUSSY TRAP 1-5
By **Nene Capri**

DIRTY DNA
By **Blaque**

SANCTIFIED AND HORNY
by **XTASY**

BOOKS BY LDP'S CEO, CA$H

TRUST IN NO MAN
TRUST IN NO MAN 2
TRUST IN NO MAN 3
BONDED BY BLOOD
SHORTY GOT A THUG
THUGS CRY
THUGS CRY 2
THUGS CRY 3
TRUST NO BITCH
TRUST NO BITCH 2
TRUST NO BITCH 3
TIL MY CASKET DROPS
RESTRAINING ORDER
RESTRAINING ORDER 2
IN LOVE WITH A CONVICT
LIFE OF A HOOD STAR
XMAS WITH AN ATL SHOOTER

www.ingramcontent.com/pod-product-compliance
Lightning Source LLC
LaVergne TN
LVHW020713110826
845149LV00012B/2241
9781971770246